The Circus Oasis

Robert Essig

Part One

Thursday

The ornate box looked like something that would have fit nicely in a museum of the damned. Clutched tightly in hands that hadn't seen a proper washing in weeks, it was clear where the discoloration and grime on the box had come from.

Katherine had been living on the streets for the past decade or so, only it wasn't really the streets that she frequented. An old school hobo that rode the rails into towns with more desirable weather, much like geese that fly south for winter, Katherine spent half the year in Slab City, a plot of desert in Southern California on the outskirts of the Salton Sea where it was legal to live off the grid in anything from a tent to a motorhome or even a shack made of refuse. The place had its own governing body right down to an unofficial mayor and a group of bruisers who acted as the "law," though the only real rule of Slab City was that there were no rules.

Katherine had some friends she lived with during her stints in the lawless desert city, but none of them had a car. As in the real world, people tended to stick with their own, which meant the hitchers found a common bond in talking about life on the road. In contrast, those who had their own transportation could hardly relate to the woes of thumbing for a ride or dealing with the often times odd individuals who still picked up hitchhikers these days.

The walk to the Salton Sea was grueling, even at three in the morning. There wasn't a cloud in the sky, so the walk started out cold, but soon enough Katherine's blood was flowing, and she began to sweat. But that didn't matter. Getting the box to the Salton Sea was all that mattered at that moment.

The box was made of any variety of wood; hickory, pine, cedar, whatever was handy. Katherine couldn't say for sure, but she thought it was hobo art, something of a lost form in the modern day of the back-alley bum who pisses himself and shits in dark corners. It was one of three that she owned. Three of the only possessions Katherine had from her previous life, hauled around for the past ten years through thick and thin. Pieces had broken off of the boxes, but they were still fine works of art, at least in Katherine's eyes, and that's why she was so perplexed by the sudden decision to take this particular box to the Salton Sea and let it go.

No, it wasn't a decision. It was an urge, uncontrollable, a magnetism she had never felt before.

Sandaled feet crunched tiny tilapia bones as she approached the sulfuric-smelling water. There was a rumor amongst the people of Slab City that a massive filtration system had been built to take some of the salt out of the water. However, it still smelled of rotten eggs and dead fish, the latter, intermittently visible at the edge of the shore, like foul offerings from some deep Salton Sea entity.

Katherine, feet in excruciating pain from the walk (done with no rest stops, which was insane and nearly impossible for a malnourished woman of fifty-eight years old), set the box in maybe two inches of water at the shore. To place a wooden box in water was a sin, especially after everything she had done to protect the box. Seeing it there, Katherine felt a twist of regret in her guts matched with relief, as if she had been shouldering the weight of the galaxy for about as long as she could remember. It felt good to let the thing go.

The small box began to sink into the fishbone sand. Katherine's eyes went wide and she crouched, extending her hand, but suddenly there seemed to be a barrier around the tramp art, as if touching it would send a jolt of electricity that, using the water as a conductor, would electrocute Katherine. It continued to sink into the wet sand as if something had a grip on the box and was pulling it under.

Exhaustion caught up with Katherine, and she collapsed onto the shoreline. Her breathing became shallow. Dead fish odors filled her nostrils, but she was far too wiped out to be bothered with foul aromatics. Just as her numbed mind folded into darkness a noise from behind caused her eyes to open wide, if only for a moment, before closing: a deep roiling purr from a feline far larger than your average house cat.

Chapter One

Being the first to stay in a newly renovated hotel room was a unique experience in not having to check the mattress for bedbugs or wear socks or flip-flops even at night to avoid contact with the soiled carpet. This luxury was lost on Danni Burkhead; however, her parents Mica and Erin were impressed enough to stifle the almost constant arguing that pretty much spoiled the entire trip from Los Angeles to the Salton Sea.

Danni had her headphones on for most of the drive, playing games on her tablet and watching videos on YouTube. It blocked out the arguing well enough. She didn't completely know what her parents had been at each other about, but she figured it had something to do with her father losing his job. She'd heard words like nepotism, cheap labor, and "those goddamned illegal immigrants." Still, she didn't really understand why it was that her mother and father couldn't just talk through their problems and work things out, like they told her to do when she became frustrated with her homework. Sometimes they behaved in ways they would frown upon were they to see her reflect such behaviors. Danni was pretty sure the word for that was hypocrite.

"This is really nice, isn't it?" Mica said. He deposited his suitcase on the bed closest to the air conditioner. He was what he liked to refer to as a "hot sleeper," whereas Erin couldn't sleep without being tucked under the covers. Sleep temperature was fodder for future arguments, especially since the argument bar had been set so low. Mica was trying to lighten the mood. He was good at that, though often he put it on too thick and came off almost cheesy.

"It *should* be nice," Erin said, taking in her surroundings like an art critic at a bad opening. "The place was completely remodeled."

Danni noted the tone in her mother's voice. The sarcasm. The bitter, bitter sarcasm that said her mother wasn't finished with the argument, that one wrong word from her father could resurrect the bickering that Danni hoped would be left in the car. She wasn't used to watching her parents behave like this, but she was beginning to make note of their habits, like children do. Most of the fighting was done behind closed doors at home, and Danni's parents really didn't argue a lot—at least not until recently.

Mica sat on the edge of the bed, facing the air conditioner. He reached out and then thought better of adjusting the temperature. "Pretty hot out there," he said, priming Erin. "We should probably crank this thing up now before the room heats up, don't you think?"

Erin looked at the air conditioner and cocked her head (another little tick Danni had mentally filed away). "You'd think they'd have put in central air. Isn't that what the new hotels in Vegas are doing?"

Mica shrugged. "This isn't Vegas, honey. We're in a circus-themed hotel in the Salton Sea. We're lucky we don't have a clown fanning us off." He flashed a goofy smile, something he did in hopes that his gesture of good cheer would be reciprocated. He was trying too hard.

Erin dismissed her husband's weak attempt at a joke. "Seems like central air would be more sensible with this heat and all."

"Well, at least we know the AC won't cut out since we're the first to use it. Look at how shiny and new this thing is. Not even a speck of dirt on it."

Erin finally sloughed off her purse onto a stationary table that was obviously purchased second-hand, considering the dings and dents showing through the new layer of varnish. If she had a snotty remark about the furniture, she kept it to herself.

Danni's tablet was forgotten about as she became immersed in the décor. The wallpaper was made up of vertical stripes like on the outside of a circus tent. The pictures, screwed to the wall to deter thievery, showcased reprints of circus themes, one displaying a trapeze act, another with a ringleader taunting a lion (he armed with a whip and wooden chair; the lion armed with a snarl and sharp teeth). The picture above the wall-mounted flat-screen was a watercolor of barred cells containing large animals like elephants and tigers. The colors were muted and sad, and somehow the artist captured a sense of desperation in the animals' expressions.

Noting his daughter's fascination with that particular picture, and perhaps acknowledging a shift in her demeanor, Mica said, "They don't do that anymore, you know, keeping animals in cages like that. It was a simpler time. People didn't know any better."

The word archaic came to Danni, but she wasn't sure that was what she wanted to say. "They look sad."

Mica put his hands on his daughter's shoulders, standing behind her. He knelt to speak into her ear. "You know that's not what they do here, right?"

Danni nodded. "I kind of wonder what it would have been like, you know, with the real animals."

"Well, honey, I only went to a circus maybe once when I was a kid, and I don't really remember. What I remember were the two motorcycle riders riding in a cage that was a big ball. I remember thinking that they were going to crash, how could they not?"

"I've got to use the bathroom," Danni said.

"Be my guest, and know that you, little girl, are the first to christen the holy porcelain throne of room . . . Uh, what room are we in again?"

"635," Erin said, now flipping through some pamphlets that were lying atop the stationary desk.

"What's christen mean?" Danni asked.

Mica raised his eyebrows. "It means you're the very first one."

Danni made a strange face of amused confusion and shrugged. "Yay, I guess?"

Both Mica and Erin laughed at their daughter's response, which cheered Danni up from the dampener that the Burkhead family started this vacation with. Once Danni was in the bathroom, Mica took Erin's hand and spoke to her softly so that maybe their daughter wouldn't eavesdrop. "Look, let's just try to forget about my job, just for this week. It's Danni's birthday. I can tell she's a little edgy because of how much we bickered on the way here. We already paid for the room, so that's covered. We can find inexpensive alternatives for our meals."

"How much did it cost to fill up the tank? Gas is over three dollars a gallon right now. Just driving out here and back is killing us."

"Shhh. Honey, I know, but we're doing this for Danni, remember? We're here, so let's enjoy it."

Erin took a deep breath. "For Danni. But when we get back, I expect you to start looking for a union or maybe a government job. Something with benefits, a retirement—"

"Yeah, yeah, I know. I heard you the first fifteen times in the car." He raised his eyebrows pleadingly to let her know he was trying to be playful rather than condescending.

Erin's cold stare remained. "But are you going to do that? We can't live on what I make, and I can't go back to college, not now. You need to work for a company that's going to protect your job."

The lock on the bathroom door clicked.

"That's the last I want to hear about it, 'kay?" Mica gave a weak smile and lifted his eyebrows as if inviting his wife to mimic him. "We're on vacation."

Erin nodded and managed a smile. "For Danni."

Danni came out beaming. "Wow! They even have circus wall-paper in the bathroom. It has little pictures of clowns and acrobats and lions and elephants. It's soooo cool."

Mica and Erin chuckled, both admiring the innocence and excitement Danni couldn't hold back if the little girl tried. She was ten years old, crazy about animals, and was beyond thrilled when her parents surprised her with a birthday gift that was this trip to the Circus Oasis Hotel, completely remodeled after closing down over thirty years ago. Back when Mica and Erin had planned the trip he was a superintendent for Christian Brothers Construction, one of Los Angeles's premier commercial and residential construction companies. He was pulling in a cool hundred fifty grand a year, which provided all the amenities a family could wish for, including vacations, an RV, and a boat. But, like so many others who fell on hard times back in 2010 in the midst of the recession, it took one bad day to show Mica what devastation felt like. They couldn't swing the mortgage on Erin's paycheck, much less two car payments and the boat and RV (both of which were sold once Mica realized that landing a job that paid what he'd been earning wasn't going to happen overnight).

It was good to be away from the house, from the city that wanted to cannibalize the very people whose tax money paved the roads and fixed the pipes. The Salton Sea wasn't exactly the type of place Mica longed to vacation at, but changes had been underway for some time to resurrect what had once been a thriving vacation destination. Mica and Erin had always thought of the Salton Sea as a hot, miserable desert that smelled of rotting fish and despair. When they heard the Circus Oasis was being remodeled and massive desalination plants had been built, the images at the Salton Sea visitor's center seemed plausible. The stories Mica's uncle used to tell about the heyday of fishing and boating and fun just might be coming back for a new generation to enjoy.

Danni sat on the bed furthest from the air conditioner, playing with a set of little magnetized balls that were all the rage amongst young kids (enough so that emergency rooms were seeing their share of intestinal problems concerning ingested magnets twisting up little kids' guts), when the ring of little gray balls rolled off the bed and onto the floor where they separated and scattered out of sight. The little girl slid off the bed and took to her hands and knees in search of the tiny links of her magnet train.

"Oh, Danni," Erin said, "get off the floor. Hotel floors are filthy."

Mica chuckled. "Oh hell, get on down there and roll around a bit."

Erin looked at him like he just assaulted a puppy.

He raised his eyes in that way he did when he was joking around. "This carpet is cleaner than ours, remember?"

Erin smirked. "Oh, thanks. You trying to say I don't clean the house good enough?"

Danni found one of the magnetized balls, placed it on the bed, and then thrust her arm under the nightstand. "I can't find the other one," she said.

"We'll find it, honey," her father said. "Don't worry. It couldn't have gone far."

"Wait a minute. There's something under here."

Erin and Mica exchanged worried glances. Finding something under the nightstand in a hotel wouldn't be surprising at all, but they were the first to check into room 635.

"Here, let me see, honey," Erin said, motherly instincts kicking in. *Could be a syringe or a razor blade after all, even in a remodeled hotel*, she thought.

"I got it," Danni said as she pulled her arm from beneath the nightstand.

Erin opened her mouth to protest as the little girl's hand emerged with an object unique enough to suck the air out of the room. Even the dreaded syringe would have made more sense however upsetting *that* would have been.

Danni beamed, "Wow! It's, it's—"

Mica's face scrunched up. "It's an animal tooth?"

Chapter Two

It was a large canine, the kind of tooth that, along with the other three in some mammal's mouth, would have been threatening matched with a snarl.

Erin didn't quite yank the tooth from Danni's hand as forcefully as she wanted to, but irrational fears of disease plagued her mind. She had told Danni not to pick up stray feathers or play with field mice for fear of plague and bird flu. For all she knew, a random tooth could be carrying something equally devastating.

"But mom," Danni said as the tooth was extracted from her grasp.

"We don't know where this came from," Erin said, examining the odd find. "What do you think, Mica?"

Erin handed Mica the tooth. He examined it with equal scrutiny. "Well, looks like the tooth of a large cat, I guess. Not particularly collectable or sought after, as far as I know, at least. Question is, what the hell is it doing in here?"

Erin nodded in agreement.

"Like, a house cat?" Danni said. And then beamed: "Can I keep it? Can I?"

Erin and Mica looked at each other as if trying to speak telepathically so their daughter wouldn't be privy to their thoughts on the subject.

"I don't know," Mica said. "That's an awfully strange thing to find, even in a hotel called the Circus Oasis."

Erin shook her head. "It's just plain out weird. I think we should go to the front desk and get to the bottom of this."

Danni pouted. "Awww mommmm."

Mica nodded in agreement with his wife. "Well, it *is* strange."

After triple-checking that they were in possession of key cards, they all took to the hallway where they ran into a loud woman. She wasn't saying anything, but loud in her bright orange t-shirt with sporadic tiger print and black pedal pushers that hinted at her age. She wore her hair in a refined bouffant that showed off her earrings—were they little dream catchers? —quite nicely. A pair of prescription glasses hung around her neck on a piece of fabric that looked like snakeskin. She stood at a door, struggling with her keycard. In addition to the suitcase at her feet were several plastic storage boxes.

"Having trouble?" Mica said as the Burkheads approached the woman on their way to the elevator.

She looked up and as if in the presence of her savior. "You know what? I remember the good ol' days when all you needed was a key to open a damn door, you know? I don't know what it is, but these keycards always trip me up."

"Here," Mica offered, "Let me see." He handed the large tooth over to Erin. The older woman's eyes locked onto the incisor with obvious curiosity. Mica said, "You see it has these arrows. That's the end that goes into the door. Arrows down, I think. You have to push the card in and hold it there until the red, see that, until the red turns green." The door chimed, bringing the older woman's attention back to Mica rather than the gleaming white tooth. Mica opened the door.

"Well, look at that," the woman said. "For a minute there I thought they messed up again."

"Again?" Erin's eyebrows rose.

The woman sighed. "There was a problem with my reservation. The place is just about booked solid for the grand opening. I get in here and they tell me I don't have a reservation. Now, I always print out my receipts for physical proof. I pull that out and things get interesting." She lowered her voice as if someone within earshot was listening. "I tell you, the folks running this place could have better people skills, particularly for a grand opening. He was so rude! He actually told me that I could have faked the receipt. Can you believe that? I say to him, 'do I look like the kind of woman who knows how to do that sort of thing? And why would I?'"

"What happened?" Erin said.

"They changed my room. Could have done that in the first place, you know? Hey," her neck craned, and her eyes zeroed in on the tooth in Erin's hand, "what have you got there?"

Erin, noticing the woman's intent stare, lifted the tooth slowly as if confused. "This?"

"Yes," the woman nodded.

"Strangest thing," Mica said. "We found it in our room."

The woman reared her head back exaggeratedly. An action that matched her flamboyant attire. "You don't say. Would you mind . . .?" She held out her hand as if expecting them to submit the tooth to her in confidence, and why not?

Erin handed it over. The woman grabbed her glasses and placed them on the bridge of her nose, tilting her head up the way people do to look down through glasses that are clearly prescribed for nearsightedness. She raised her eyes above the glasses and looked at Erin. "You say you found this in your room?"

Erin nodded.

"I hope I get to keep it," Danni said.

The woman looked down at the little girl and formed a generous smile. "And who are you, young lady?"

The little girl looked to her parents as if seeking approval to talk to this woman. Stranger danger and all that. Erin gave her daughter a reassuring smile. "Danni Burkhead," she beamed to the older woman.

"Isn't that a nice name. I'm Bette DeAnza."

"Good to meet you, Bette." Mica held out his hand to shake. "I'm Mica, and this is my wife, Erin."

Bette shook his hand and said, "This is very curious."

"Just some animal tooth, I think. Probably a large cat. Weird it was in our room, though."

Bette shook her head. "Not just any large cat though." She chewed her lip in thought, head tilted up as she looked through the lenses of the glasses resting on the tip of her nose. Her eyes darted up at the trio, who watched her as if seeking some kind of explanation regarding her apparent expertise in animal dentistry.

"Oh, I'm sorry," Bette said and smiled. "I didn't properly introduce myself. I'm a zoologist. Here observing the wildlife around the Salton Sea. I've been out several times since the desalination plants were installed. I'm a part of a group who have been tasked with monitoring the area to see how the desalination of the sea is affecting the wildlife, particularly the massive die-offs of the tilapia that the Salton Sea has been known for."

The elevator door dinged down the hall, releasing a small explosion of laughter and voices as a tight group of people exited one by one. The commotion kind of fractured their conversation.

"It was great meeting you, Bette," Erin said. "We better get down there and see what's up with the tooth. It's just so . . . weird."

Bette handed the tooth back to Erin. The look in her eyes said that she would have liked to hold onto it a bit longer, maybe investigate it, find out exactly what species of animal it came from.

"Good luck," she said. "That guy at the desk has about as much charisma as a tilapia rotting in the desert sun."

Erin offered a knowing look that came off like a pity smile. Mica said, "Oh, we've been acquainted with the charm of the desk clerk. Nothing like a warm welcome to a grand opening, right?"

Bette nodded. "See you around."

A line of customers in the lobby waited patiently with suitcases and bags, collectively thankful for the air-conditioned relief from the desert heat outside. The grand opening had funneled more people into the Salton Sea than had been seen since the place was a respected tourist destination back in the seventies.

The front desk, tucked against the far end of the lobby opposite the wall of glass doors that fed out to the parking lot, was flanked from one wall to the other with several computer monitors, though only one was in use from which the growing line stretched.

"We shouldn't have to wait in this line," Mica said. It didn't take much for him to become agitated. "There should be a customer service desk or something."

"They should have more people working the desk today," Erin said. "I'm sure most of these people made reservations. The hotel should be prepared."

Mica sighed. "Come on, we're not waiting in line."

He led the way to the front desk, Erin and Danni following, where he said to the desk clerk, with a smile and soft voice, "Could we please see someone. We have a question about our room."

The clerk, a short, lean man with dark hair and a steely gaze, looked at Mica as if he asked to have a leather-clad gimp sent up on a food trolley. "We're short-staffed today," he said.

Mica reared back, brow furled. "Short staffed? Today? It's the grand opening."

"Re-opening," the desk clerk corrected.

"Whatever, look, we need to speak with someone, maybe a manager. Don't tell me there isn't a manager around here somewhere."

The desk clerk had completely stopped helping the family who had been checking in when Mica came up to the front desk, as if he could only perform one task at a time and had to dedicate all of his efforts to that solitary task lest he lose focus and have to start all over again.

"You can wait here. My manager should be back soon."

"Can't you call him?"

Someone in line groaned. Mica turned, flashing a glare at the crowd just in case the groaner was upset with him. It wasn't so much an intimidation tactic, but rather that his opinion on society had been deteriorating as of late, and he felt like he was always under the scrutiny of someone's ire.

"He's a busy, busy man. If you would like to talk to him, you need to be patient. He will be back."

"Patient?"

"Honey," Erin said, "let's just wait. You're holding up the line."

"*I'm* holding up the line?"

Danni stood there behind her parents, watching them and wondering what was so bad about finding a big ol' cat tooth in their room. She certainly didn't see anything wrong with it. She couldn't wait until this whole scene her father was making blew over and they finally released the tooth back to her, for she was confident that's how this would end. It's not like they found the big cat (tiger, lion, fat house cat?) in their room. She did think that would be kind of cool, though.

The Burkheads waited in silence for the manager, silence save for Danni's constant questions about the lobby's décor and the future of her enamel discovery. She was young enough to be fascinated with a thing such as a pearly incisor, not yet fully understanding that if it were poached (even her father wasn't sure if people poached the teeth from lions and tigers), that would be a very bad thing. She knew that poachers were evil people who hunted majestic animals for game, and though the idea of having a deer head or antelope head hanging on the wall was disgusting, she was transfixed with the tooth. She saw it as a sort of talisman, and she wanted to hold onto it for the rest of the trip like a good luck charm.

Erin was patient with her daughter, answering questions and engaging the little girl, though Mica was fit to burst, and what for? A tooth? Yes, it was peculiar, but was it worth jeopardizing the entire trip?

Finally, a man came through a door that must have led to a staff area. He wasn't much taller than the desk clerk, but considerably greasier, as if he lathered up in olive oil before putting on his suit. His hair was thinning on top, but he still had enough for a pathetic comb-over, pasted to his shiny forehead by the thin sheen of olive oil. His eyebrows were bushy and thick (he probably wished some of that hair would have grown out of his head rather than above his eyes). At sight of the Burkheads waiting at the front desk away from the line of people with bags and suitcases, he stopped and looked them over as if they were out of place. The stern, clamped features on his face (he looked like a man who hadn't laughed in many a year, if ever) didn't so much as move, just the eyes like a robot examining for potential danger. His mustache was so thick and bristly it was hard to see the slit in his lipless mouth when he spoke.

"Is there a problem?" The man had the faintest of accents, the type that comes from decades in America speaking English in public, but speaking his native tongue at home. Mica couldn't tell where the man hailed from. Greece, the Middle East, a Slavic country, Mica had no clue and was too incensed about the wait and the poor customer service to pick apart the finer details of the man's accent for a more accurate diagnosis.

The question caught Mica off guard, for he realized at that moment, face to face with a man who clearly had a great deal of stress and far more to deal with in the opening of a hotel, that what he was going to say would turn out to be quite a minor complaint. Suddenly Mica felt small under this man's gaze, and he realized that he'd become so worked up due to the stress he was dealing with in his own life.

Though the lobby was cool and comfortable, sweat broke out on Mica's brow. He glanced sidelong to Erin, who looked upon him disapprovingly (damn how he hated that look on her), and then took a deep breath and let it out in a way he hoped would articulate, without words, how minute his complaint was. "I'm sorry to bother you, but something strange has happened."

The man behind the desk didn't say a word. He stood as stoic as ever, like a stern father looking for a reason to have an outburst at his frightened child.

Mica continued, "My daughter found this under the nightstand." He handed over the tooth. The man behind the desk didn't make an immediate gesture to grab it. He did not so much as move, but his eyes shifted downward as Mica, realizing that there would be no handoff, set the tooth on the counter.

The man stared at the object, his face shifting so slightly it could have been molded by invisible hands. He made an audible exhalation of breath through his bulbous nose, unfolded his arms, and picked up the tooth. He made a spectacle out of examining the thing, looking at it from all angles, twisting it around in his hands, and then he smiled. It was a self-assured and hazardous smile, the kind you wouldn't want to be on the opposite side of in certain situations. "A misplaced bit of décor," he said. "That's all. It's no problem."

Erin sighed. "Jeez, Mica, you should have thought of that. Now here we are wasting this man's time."

Mica had a blank look on his face. He felt foolish and ashamed of his anger, of the scene that he almost made in the lobby, and for what? A piece of décor that had probably fallen on the floor unnoticed by the interior decorators.

"Can I have it?" Danni asked. Her question broke the awkward silence; the answer broke her heart.

"No. Room decorations are not cheap. I will find out who is responsible for this and make sure things are fixed." His face had darkened a bit, and then that absurd smile crept back in, mischievous and haughty. His eyes shifted from the little girl to her father. "Anything else?"

Mica shook his head. "No. Thanks."

The Burkhead family walked through the lobby towards the elevator. Mica felt stupid and ashamed, but regardless he didn't like the man at the desk. His name tag said Elric Lazar. As the elevator doors opened, Mica thought about the name and pondered its origin. He also paid close attention to the décor. By the time they were back in their room unpacking, Mica couldn't help but notice that there were no decorations in the lobby, the hallway, or in their room that were created of actual harvested animal teeth or other trophies.

Chapter Three

Bette DeAnza felt alive even while her feet crunched on the bones of so many long-dead fish in the screaming sun of a noonday desert. Having been to the Salton Sea before, she knew what to expect, but now that she was here with the sole purpose of collecting samples, she felt almost overwhelmed.

After the desalination plants went online there were years of clean-up and reams of red tape with regard to environmental concerns. The Salton Sea had been a veritable soup of dead fish and birds and yearly algae growth resulting in a horrible stench that could be detected miles away, especially in whipping desert winds. Years ago, Sonny Bono spent bookoo bucks investing in what he thought would be the next Palm Springs, a desert oasis with water sports, fishing, and all the sun you could soak into your skin. Sonny became the unofficial mayor of the Salton Sea, and for about a decade there it seemed as if his vision would have longevity.

Then the fish and bird die-offs began.

There's nothing like the aroma of dead fish to enhance a relaxing vacation.

Bette collected fish bones in a plastic bag and used a Sharpie marker to tag the bag with an approximate location and date. She sought out newer fish bones rather than the sun-baked variety that would easily crumble in her fingers. During the clean-up process after the installation of the desalination plants, it was quickly realized that removing all of the fish bones would be a futile effort, considering that's what composed half of the sand at the water's edge.

In concert with the development of desalination plants, canals were constructed to collect runoff from nearby Imperial Valley farms and redirect overflow from the Tijuana River. In the nineties, fish and bird die-offs hit record levels and, until California legislation came up with a bill to fund the multi-million-dollar project, the die-offs appeared to have no end. It was a horrible cycle that had the potential to bring certain protected species close to extinction. The process was fairly simple, with several unknowns. Due to the rich runoff from the Imperial Valley farms and pollution from the Tijuana River compounded with the extreme desert heat, the perfect conditions were set for algae blooms that would spread across the water like massive streaks of pink paint. Quite amazing, perhaps even beautiful, to see from above, but deadly for the millions of tilapia that would then struggle for space and oxygen in the desert sea. Massive die-offs would then occur, and the fish would wash up on shore in the thousands. Migrating birds would then feast on the dead fish, on the maggots, and disease was spread, in turn causing massive bird die-offs.

Though the birds were dying from a variety of diseases such as avian cholera, Newcastle disease, avian botulism, and unidentified ailments, the algae blooms were often under scrutiny. The theory was that if the fish die-offs were prevented and the quality of the water was brought back to where it had been in the seventies, the birds would be safe, and people could begin to look at the Salton Sea as a tourist destination once again.

As for Bette, she thought the opening of the Circus Oasis hotel was a bit premature. Well, the re-opening. Despite Sonny Bono's idea of a new Palm Springs, the Lazar family built a circus-themed hotel much like the famous Circus Circus hotel and casino in Las Vegas. Bette had heard the rumors about the infamous Circus Oasis. The cruel and unusual treatment of their animals—starvation, malnutrition, heatstroke. It was with a heavy heart that Bette was even staying in a place that had treated majestic animals such as lions, elephants, and tigers the way they had purportedly done. It was the seventies, but that was no excuse for cruelty. Being that the Lazar family still ran the place, Bette had been short with them when checking in. She wanted nothing to do with that family and their hotel. If not for the sake of environmental research, she wouldn't be caught dead there.

Well, Bette thought, *at least they're not allowed to have animals in their circus anymore.*

She came across a dead bird at the shoreline, gently swaying with the water. A gull-billed tern. Bette took in a deep breath. Even one dead bird was something to be concerned about. It could be natural causes, could be disease, could be anything. Bette used a gloved hand to grab the bird and placed it into a plastic bag. She then tagged the bag the way she had for the fish and placed it into an ice chest she had brought along for preservation. The specimens would be kept on ice until she could deliver them to the private agency she worked for in San Diego.

Though there had been reams of files containing what seemed like endless environmental reports before the desalination plants were built, it was well known that money could grease the skids and move a project along regardless of certain hazards. Bette had been hired by a third party to take part in a private investigation.

This would be a great trip if all Bette found were some recent fish bones and a dead bird. Last time, several months ago, she found a dozen dead birds of four different species, and she counted thirty-four fish, though she had only collected ten of them to be dissected and studied.

"Look mom!" a youthful voice said, averting Bette from her deep thoughts. "It's the lady from the hallway."

Recognizing the little girl whose father had helped Bette with the keycard earlier, she smiled and waved. The Burkhead family walked toward the shore, though they weren't carrying beach chairs and fishing poles. They didn't even have flip-flops on like your average beachgoer. Bette wondered how long it would be before the stigma of the Salton Sea wore off enough for people to trust the waters.

"Hello you," Bette said to Danni. She crouched down a bit to be sure that Danni knew she was addressing her. Though they had only met briefly in the hallway, she felt a sort of kinship with the little girl. In some strange way that could hardly be ascertained during a five-minute meeting, Bette saw a little bit of herself in Danni, as she too was once that little girl who had an affinity for animals. Were Bette oblivious to the past that haunted the Circus Oasis, she too would have been thrilled to be there.

"Hello, Miss Bette," Danni said after breaking away from her parents and jogging down the beach.

Bette greeted the girl with a generous smile. "Well, fancy running into you here. How are you enjoying your stay so far?"

Danni was beaming. "I *love* it! Did you know there's a room that has pictures of the *real* circus animals they used to have here, like, a long time ago?"

Bette's beaming smile faltered only a little bit. *I bet the photos don't show the reality of how those poor animals were treated.* She firmed up her smile. "No, I didn't know."

Danni nodded. "It's *really* cool. There are banners and things from the original Circus Oasis. I can't wait until the circus. It's gonna be so fun. I just wish they still had the real animals. Wouldn't that be so cool?"

Again, Bette's smile dropped a bit. "Well, it's better for the animals now. I'm sure the new show will be just fine."

"Better for the animals?"

Bette's eyes shifted to Danni's parents, almost as if seeking guidance on how to proceed, or perhaps confirmation that she proceed at all. No one liked preachy strangers, and it wasn't her place to lecture their daughter.

Erin offered a sort of sad, sympathetic expression and then knelt to her daughter's level. "Sometimes circus animals were mistreated. That's why there is a law against using live animals in modern circuses. It's progress. Years ago, there was something called a freak show in carnivals that exploited people with disabilities. It wasn't very nice, but we know better now."

Danni pouted her lips and tilted her head in a way that showed she was accepting these terms. "Well, I guess that's okay. As long as the animals like it better this way."

"Oh, they do," said Bette. "They most certainly do."

"Are you going to the Big Top Show, Miss Bette?"

Bette shook her head. "You know what? I never did like circuses. Even as a little girl I remember the first circus I went to. Something about those beautiful animals being tethered and made to perform rubbed me wrong." She looked up over the heads of Danni and her parents to see the Circus Oasis Hotel looming in the distance, the canvas tent beside it. She nodded. "But this one, I think I'll give it a shot. If anything, it will be interesting to see how they pull it off with the mechanical animals."

"I hope we see you there," Danni said with a smile that could not be denied.

"I'm sure we'll run into one another again."

Mica cleared his throat. It was a method of gaining someone's attention that, frankly, irritated his wife. "Well," he said, "I guess we should head over to Bombay Beach before we roast out here."

"The beach is quite nice now," Bette said, "but I would stay away from the little neighborhood of mobile homes. They don't take kindly to strangers, or so I've heard. Takes a certain type of person to live all these years next to a lake that smelled like dead fish, you know?"

Mica nodded. "Thanks for the tip. I've seen Bombay Beach somewhere on TV, a documentary or something. I think parts have been used in photoshoots."

"It's changed a lot since then. It's not nearly as dilapidated. The broken docks and several mobile homes that were ruined years ago when the waters rose have been removed. Just think, if the hotel does well and some of the old restaurants reopen, those mobile homes might actually be worth something."

Mica chuckled. "I don't know about that. They're in pretty rough shape. Looks like a good wind will knock most of them down."

"Well, whoever owns the land will see an increase in equity. That is, just so long as this revamping of the Salton Sea actually brings people back. It's gonna take more than a circus-themed hotel, that's for sure."

"Oh, I'm sure developers have it all mapped out. The restaurant's supposed to open by the end of the month. I'm sure that little liquor store I saw on the way in is benefiting from the hotel already."

Bette's mouth parted slightly like she wanted to say something else, but she shook off her thoughts and they said their goodbyes. The Burkheads sauntered off toward Bombay Beach, leaving a series of dimples in the fishbone sand.

Deciding that she had about enough of the heat for the time being, and feeling lunchtime hunger pangs, Bette decided to bring the ice chest up to her room and see what kind of delicacies were offered in the Big Top restaurant just off the lobby in the hotel. With the restaurant down the road a month away from opening, it really didn't matter what they were offering in the hotel. It would have to do, or else Bette take a half-hour drive around the lake and eat at Red Earth Casino over off the 86 on the other side of the Salton Sea.

Grabbing the handle of her ice chest Bette took two steps toward the hotel when she saw something in the sand that took her aback. She tilted her head like a curious dog, and then took off her sunglasses. She felt the brightness of the sun on her eyes, but what she saw in the sand remained. Bette knelt down, mouth agape. Sun reflected off the bright white sand, but nothing could cause her eyes to close in that moment, for imprinted across the shore of the Salton Sea were animal tracks. Some kind of large cat. The type typically found in an African tundra or the zoo.

Or a circus.

Chapter Four

The outside of the circus tent where the Big Top Show would be performed was striped vertically in red and white. There were points around the tent that imitated the poles that once held up traditional circus tents above, which was another slope to the apex where a massive support the size of a telephone pole was topped with a huge flag that said: THE LAZAR FAMILY CIRCUS. The other poles were topped with colorful flags and streamers from one to another with strips of color that whipped in the desert winds. It was an exact replica of a bona fide circus tent, but built permanently to withstand the elements, though no one could say how long the colors of the flags and the stripes would hold up to the damaging sun rays.

Inside, Tracy Lazar and her daughter Eve were at each other's throats again, something that had been happening more often. Tracy thought Eve's teen years were bad, but that was nothing more than a primer for what was to become of a daughter who seemed to have come out of the womb with attitude. At twenty-four, Eve didn't have the know-it-all assuredness that many other twenty-somethings possessed, just raw attitude that bordered on anger and straight-out meanness. Secretly, Tracy blamed this on the Lazar Clan (as she liked to refer to them), but she would never say that to Edgar. She knew what she was getting into when she married Edgar. But he wasn't like the rest of his family.

Eve rolled her eyes (probably for, like, the twentieth time since she and her mother decided to inspect the circus for tomorrow night's inaugural Big Top Show). "These are totally stupid." She ran a finger across the plastic teeth in the mouth of an animatronic tiger. "No one's gonna buy it."

Tracy, who was busy with a rag polishing the gleaming painted animals, regarded her daughter like a plague. "Everyone knows these aren't real animals. It's not like we're trying to fool anyone. Christ, girl, hasn't anyone told you that if you don't have anything good to say—"

"Don't say anything at all?" Eve raised her eyebrows, which caused the three piercings above her right eye to gleam as light from the intricate setup above the circus ring caught the metal. "You've been saying that shit to me since I learned how to say fuck you. If I listened to that kind of shit advice everyone would think I was a fucking mute."

"Might not be such a bad thing, you buttoning your lip from time to time."

Eve made a goofy, sarcastic face. "Yeah, well, FUCK that."

Tracy slumped her shoulders and dropped her hands to her sides. "You're a real piece of work, you know that?"

An oh-so-familiar smirk. "Not a day goes by you don't remind me."

Continuing her final polish on the new mechanical circus animals, Tracy wondered what her ungrateful daughter was doing here. Over many a fight it was established that Eve would have to help out with the hotel if she wanted to continue to live under Tracy and Edgar's roof. They hoped a steady job would straighten Eve out a bit, but her sour persona was as strong and distasteful as ever. Tracy could hardly stand to be in the presence of her daughter for more than, say, five minutes before the bickering started, and if she didn't start it Eve certainly would.

Eve examined each animal as if looking for runs on the glossy lacquer finish, running her black and red fingernails over them, kind of like Freddy Krueger taunting frightened children. She tilted her head to the left and then the right in a gesture that, to Tracy, who was well acquainted with the mischievous ways of her sullen daughter, was rife with thoughtless consideration, the type that typically led to slander and/or mockery.

Stopping in front of the lion at the center of the ring, Eve looked up at her mother, her chin-length bob covering half of her face in an array of color spread out beneath platinum blonde like some exotic rendering of a male peacock's splayed-out feathers. "It's not going to work, you know. All of this . . . this fake shit. People don't want this."

Tracy continued to polish a beautiful horse that looked as if it could grace an ornate carousel. The piece was sparkling, but Tracy continued polishing to occupy her hands and mind, else she may lash out at her ungrateful offspring. She knew what Eve was doing. She was just trying to get the better of her, and dammit, the girl was succeeding. Through clenched teeth, Tracy said, "How the hell would you know what people want?"

Eve looked up as if considering something. "The outside looks like a real circus tent, but in here it looks like something else. All these air conditioning units, the lighting." She chortled. "The fake animals. No one is going to come back." Eve shook her head. "This is forgettable. The Yelp reviews are going to blow."

Tracy dropped her rag on the ground (it was dirt like a tradi- tional circus—not sand like on the Salton Sea, but dirt that had been trucked in and packed hard). "Look, you know damn well it's not just about the animals. There's much more to the show, and as we grow, it will become even bigger. People won't be coming to see our mechanized lions and tigers."

"Grammy Val says if you're not having real animals, you should at least bring back the freak show. That would be fucking cool."

Tracy picked the rag up and snapped it in the air to get the dust off of it. "You know we couldn't do that if we wanted. Exploiting people with deformities is neither entertaining nor commendable."

"Yeah right. People love that shit. Makes them feel better about themselves to see a pinhead and bearded woman. You got rosacea, and you see a guy with goddamned scales on his body, you don't feel like such a freak for a little redness, you know? It's like watching a car wreck in slow motion. People always stop for a car wreck."

Eve, lingering in the center of the circus ring, spotted a coiled whip on a stool. She grabbed it and allowed the length to unfurl, the tip lying on the ground. Tracy swallowed hard, frozen in place for a second before realizing her mistake and beginning another task.

Eve grinned. "Wouldn't it be something if we could show people a real car wreck? They'd pay for that shit too, you know it."

With her back to Eve, Tracy said, "You're morbid."

"Naw, it's nostalgia. I just want to see a real-to-life circus."

Tracy turned. "Nostalgia? What do you know about freak shows? You've never even seen one."

"Grammy Val told me about them. I've seen the movie *Freaks.* I've watched documentaries."

Tracy was pleased to have Eve on the defensive. "It's cruel, and people don't want to see that as much as you think. Certainly not the type who we want staying in the hotel. I told you before that we will eventually get a troupe of performance artists. A sword swallower, a tattooed man (used to call them an illustrated man way back), people with strange body modifications, even flesh hook suspension."

"Weaksauce."

Eve gripped the whip handle tight and lifted it above her head. She brought it down in a quick snap that startled Tracy, who stood there with her mouth agape. "Where did you learn that?"

After coiling the whip and placing it back atop the stool, Eve said, "Grammy Val, who else? She was the best."

Tracy nodded. She couldn't disagree. Edgar's mother had been a hell of a performer in her day. No woman around could hold an audience the way she could. No woman around would face a lion the way she did, and the damn beast seemed to be afraid of her. Tracy saw the show back in the seventies when she was a teen and had eyes for Edgar. At the time, his mother Valerie was someone to idolize up there, center ring, facing ferocious animals without a hint of fear, but Tracy had learned to despise the woman over the years. She was nothing more than a big bully. And sadistic to boot.

Tracy's eyes deepened. "You're not going out to that goddamned mountain with her, are you?"

Eve's eyes dropped. Apparently, it was more difficult for her to lie to her mother than Tracy thought. The girl was so straightforward that it was odd to see her squirm. Tracy figured Eve had lost all respect for her parents long ago, but there was still a little something there. Maybe.

After a few steps toward her daughter, Tracy hesitated. On second thought, it was better not to try and console the young woman, for she would be nothing more than insulting were Tracy to show the girl such a sign of emotion. "We had to do some pretty awful things to make ends meet all these years, especially your grandparents."

"Jesus, that's 'cause you and dad wouldn't help them. You guys were pulling in money pretty good, weren't you? Just hoarding that shit away for yourselves while the rest of the family struggled. We all know it. That's why Grammy Val hates you."

"Don't you even talk to me like that. We did what we did to get the hotel back up and running. Isn't this what your precious Grammy Val wanted? Isn't it? And don't think for one second that she would have stopped with her little roadside shows had we gave her money. She'd have blown all the cash on her damn shows rather than survival. Maybe if she put more of her focus on your grandpa he would be in better health. Ever think about that? I feel sorry for him, that he's been ignored. I just know one day Valerie's gonna wake up and he'll be cold beside her in bed, and you know what? I don't think she'll do a damn thing about it. Just leave him there until he starts to smell. Then she might, and I stress *might*, call the authorities to cart his corpse away. If she can't figure out a way to exploit him first."

Tracy threw her polishing rag on the ground and stormed out of the big top tent before Eve had a chance to retort.

The sun outside was oppressive, beating down on Tracy like a warm pillow ready to smother her. Even in distress she recognized, at that moment, just how efficient the air conditioning units cooled the big top tent. Outside of the doubt her ungrateful daughter filled her mind with, everything seemed to be falling into place for a wonderful opening night. The hotel was nearly booked solid for the weekend, the Oasis restaurant was doing good business, there weren't too many complaints about the heat, and most of all the mechanized animals were all in good working condition.

Tracy entered the hotel lobby and made a b-line for the door next to the check-in desk that led to a storage area and break lounge. Tracy needed a moment before she continued checking her lengthy list of last-minute adjustments. Holding a conversation with Eve took everything out of here these days as if Eve possessed some kind of power that could drain an individual of their passion and drive. It was kind of frightening how that daughter of hers could tear a person down in such a smooth manner like she had prepared all her life for such devastations. Tracy sighed. That's just what Eve had done, all her life. She was a miserable kid who grew into a miserable woman, and misery loves company.

Way Tracy saw it, the mechanical circus animals were a great investment. They looked amazing and the movements were far advanced to those shifty, rigid animatronics that were used in places like Chuck E. Cheese's, which were solely geared to entertain kids and poorly maintained. These animals were sleek and moved with grace, completely controlled by advanced computer electronics that gave them distinctively animalistic movement.

When Edgar and Tracy finally realized that they had the savings to convince investors to loan them lofty sums of money for this massive undertaking (the project helped along and encouraged by the construction of desalination plants), they had planned on bringing back the live animal show that the Circus Oasis had back in the seventies. Nostalgia made the past shine in retrospect, and sometimes horrors were well hidden, or even dwarfed by life events. This was true for Edgar's fond memories of the Big Top Show back in the day when his mother was ring mistress. Tracy figured he had blinders and ignored or perhaps pushed back any memories of how poorly Valerie treated the animals. During those peak years when the Salton Sea was a destination, The Great Val knew how to put on a show, and audiences were receptive. Even Tracy enjoyed the show back then. After she met Edgar and they began dating, and then her parents died in a tragic car wreck on the 8 Freeway coming down Banner Pass (a car in the opposite lane swerved to avoid what turned out to be a large piece of luggage on the road and caused a head-on collision), she was brought into the Lazar family with welcome arms. Only then did she see what really happened once the crowds left the tent. She shivered just thinking about it.

Edgar had been there for her. Even before her parents died, Tracy had fallen for Edgar. He had been a charming young man who loved the family business and had been learning the ins and outs of running a circus. He was romantic and caring in an environment that was full of tourists, vacationers, and ornery locals, which may have come from growing up in a world of whimsy. He lived on the road with the family sideshow until his parents finished construction on the original Circus Oasis Hotel and opened for business. Edgar had never attended school like other kids, had few restrictions, and certainly didn't understand a nine-to-five world. His sense of time had been molded by nighttime shows, hanging with carnies and circus performers, and growing up way too quickly. The benefit of such a lifestyle during his formidable years was that he knew how to treat a girl. He knew what to say. He knew how to behave. He also knew tragedy, having dealt with his uncle Jameson falling off the trapeze wire without a net and breaking his back; watching his mentor Jeffery Schlinski (who had always been there for him when his parents were busy running the sideshow) slowly die of cancer and yet put on the clown makeup and cheer up the kiddies every goddamn night until he physically couldn't do so any longer. When Tracy was in need after her parents died, Edgar was there for her, and he knew what to do to alleviate her pain. Through tragedy, they had developed a bond that, to this day, seemed unbreakable.

Even when their rotten daughter tried so desperately to break it.

Eve lingered in the tent, kneeling before the tigers and the lion, looking them straight in the eyes. *They have no fear,* she thought.

Eve shook her head, wild colored hair gently bobbing.

She grabbed the whip again in a clump that kept the coil together in a circle. She stepped back a few paces from the lion (the prized animal of the bunch, according to her mother, but not nearly as expensive as the mechanical elephant). Eve kept her forefinger and thumb tightly clenched around the whip's hilt and pulled her other fingers back, allowing the coiled length to drop to the ground. Grammy Val had taught her showmanship and maneuvering in a way that was seamless, a way that would give even a simple dropping of the whip pizzazz.

Pulling the whip back, eyes trained on the lion, teeth gritted. The lion didn't move, didn't so much as breath, much less roar. Eve shook her head again. *No fear is no fun.*

She brought the whip down with practiced precision. It cracked the lion right on the face leaving a stripe of black from the leather.

Eve dropped the whip, turned, and left the tent.

No, she concluded, *nothing like the real thing*.

Chapter Five

The heat didn't seem to bother Danni. On the way to Bombay Beach she would run ahead of her parents to examine something poking out of the sand, be it a rock or even fish bones, though she had better sense than to touch those.

The water's edge didn't change as they made their way to Bombay Beach, but soon enough the mobile homes came into view like rotten teeth on some massive gaping maw. Some of them were in ruins, abandoned with collapsed carports and corrugated metal peeling off the frame in sheets. The occupied mobile homes were cluttered with dusty debris and old cars that probably couldn't make it out of the Salton Sea even with a tune-up and full tank of gas. Some of the vehicles were so breaded in dust and sand they looked like they hadn't moved in years.

The Burkheads kept to the shore, but Mica and Erin's eyes were glued to the little town of squalor. There was no real sign of people except for clutter around the occupied mobile homes and the inconsistent hum of air conditioners. No one was outside getting sun, cooling off in the water, gardening (there were no gardens to be found in Bombay Beach).

"It's like a ghost town," Erin said.

They passed by a single-wide that had collapsed. The heap was covered at the edges with sand that would, over many years, develop into a dune. Mica nodded in agreement, his steps slowing as they took in a town that was as morbidly interesting as a car wreck. "A living ghost town. There are people here."

"How do they live like this?"

Mica shrugged and looked away, preferring, for the moment, to gaze upon the Salton Sea, sunbeams dancing like polished crystals on the gently swaying waters. "Hard times call for hard living, I guess. There are mobile homes all over the desert. The land is cheap. Slap down a single wide. Better than living on the streets."

Erin wrinkled her brow with a look of genuine distaste, a look one could easily misconstrue as snobbish privilege. "Seems like the electric bill would be out of control."

"Take a closer look." Mica smirked. "Half of these people have old-school air conditioners propped in windows. I don't know if that's more efficient than central air or what. I guess it doesn't take much to cool down a single wide, but you'd think the metal siding would absorb the heat, right? Maybe all the shit piled up on the sides works as insulation."

They shuffled along, trying not to gawk but unable to refrain from examining the squalor that was Bombay Beach. The plots of land closer to the water's edge were worse for wear, many of them completely vacant and others scattered with debris or the rotted skeletons of a long-ago destroyed mobile home. Timbers jutted out like sharp rib bones waiting to skewer an unsuspecting jogger. Discarded appliances were littered at random like sentient hunks of metal that seemed to be slowly consumed by greedy sands, refrigerators, and washing machines like deathtraps for unsuspecting young children.

Suddenly and without warning, Danni went into a run toward a lot with a cracked cement foundation and piles of garbage that gave it a look like maybe the locals considered it their own personal dump, or perhaps just the remains of the family who once lived there, large black trash bags of belongings that wouldn't fit in the car when they evacuated for some other form of existence. There was a stagnant puddle in the middle of the lot. That it hadn't evaporated gave off the impression that the water table was low here, perhaps a reason the lots closer to the water's edge were all in ruins.

"Danni!" Erin hoped her call alone would dissuade the little girl from whatever caught her attention enough to bolt for what was essentially a dump.

"Honey, stay away from there," Mica said.

Danni either didn't hear her parents or wasn't listening, for her speed seemed to increase. At this, Mica strode forward at an increased pace. "Danni!"

It was unusual for Danni to ignore her parents. She had been so well behaved all her life that Mica and Erin joked about how the terrible teens were going to be a doozie. Whatever had caught her attention so deeply must have been really important to her.

At the edge of the abandoned plot, Danni stopped. The eagerness she possessed fled, and her body slumped as if in the wake of some great letdown. Mica came up behind her, his rushed gait lessening at the sight of his daughter's apparent despair. "What's going on, honey? You see something over here?"

Mouth agape, Danni was momentarily lost for words. "I thought . . ." She shook her head and then looked at her father. "I thought I saw something." She shook her head. "Must have been, what do they call that, a muh-mirage."

Mica reared his head back. "A mirage, huh? It's hot out, but I don't know it's mirage hot."

Erin came up from behind Mica. "What's the rush? Where's the fire?"

Suddenly Danni looked ashamed. "Nothing, Mom."

Mica looked at his wife. "Says she saw a mirage."

Erin, concerned: "A mirage? Of what?"

Danni shook her bowed head. "Nothing."

Mica and Erin exchanged questioning looks. This sort of behavior was so unusual for Danni that they didn't know what to think. It wasn't a big deal, but Danni's response, the apparent shame she felt for seeing something that wasn't there, caught her parents off guard.

Mica cleared his throat and wiped sweat off his brow. "Honey, you must have seen something in this junk that looked like something else."

Danni continued to look at the ground as if lost in her own little trance. Mica hoped he wasn't seeing into Danni's future as a stubborn teenager who could hold a grudge and have a cold shoulder like the best of them.

Erin's patience was only half that of Mica's on a good day, and she was beginning to show the signs of reaching the point of irritation that resulted in sighs and eye-rolling. It was a good thing their daughter was so well behaved. Mica didn't know what Erin would do if they had a problem child.

Erin swallowed hard and put a hand on Danni's shoulder. "Come on, let's go back to the water." She grimaced. "This place is kinda gross, isn't it?"

Danni's body tensed under her mother's hand, and then the little girl crouched down in a swift movement. She reached out and grabbed a piece of paper that was wrinkled with water damage. She pulled it up, salt crystallized on the corners, glittering in the sun.

Erin pulled her hand back. "What have you got there?"

Danni's eyes narrowed in scrutiny of the paper. "Says something about a zoo."

"A zoo? Out here?"

Danni shrugged. "That's what it says. At a place called," she worked the first word syllabically, "Damn-na-tion Mountain."

Mica had been more interested in the ruins, but swiveled his head toward his daughter. "I've heard of a Salvation Mountain."

Danni looked up. "Really, Daddy?"

Mica nodded. "Yeah, but it's not a zoo. Or at least I've never heard anything about it being a zoo. Who puts a zoo out here in the desert anyway?"

Erin asked, "What's Salvation Mountain? Sounds like some kind of religious destination or something."

"Well, I'm not totally sure. Saw something about it on TV. If I remember correctly, it's a little mountain that has been painted with all these colors, and yes, I think there were psalms or something painted on the side of the mountain. 'God loves you' or something like that. Weird thing about that is the guy who started it (or at least I think he did) is a nudist. He encourages people to bring their old paints out, and he just slathers paint on the mountain, making shapes and religious messages. He's so sunburnt he looks like a living piece of beef jerky."

Erin looked worried, as if just talking about these diametrically opposing mountains was cause for fear. "I wonder what Damnation Mountain is."

"A zoo!" Danni beamed.

"I don't know if I want to go to a zoo at a place called Damnation Mountain."

Mica reached his hand out. "Let me see that."

Danni handed over the stained flier. Mica held it close and then pulled the paper back and forth, as if trying to get it in focus. "Jesus," he said, "looks like I really do need glasses." He squinted and read, lips moving, the words dancing in his mind rather than spoken aloud. "Hmm. Sounds like one of those old roadside attractions that used to be set up along the highways out in the desert. They would advertise it as a zoo, but really they were capturing desert animals like rattlesnakes, rabbits, lizards, scorpions and the like. Just a scam to fleece tourists and people passing through. I've never actually seen one. Probably outlawed these days."

"Fleece?" Danni said. "Like a jacket?"

This comment resulted in a pleasant laughter that broke through the haze of despair that had set in (the despair probably induced more by the general squalor of Bombay Beach than a flier about some roadside scam).

Erin said, "Fleece also means to take money or goods from someone through unsavory means. If that makes any sense."

Danni nodded. "Yeah, I get it."

"I don't condone littering," Mica said, "but I think we're going to just leave this flier where we found it." He offered a goofy smile, one that usually elicited a chuckle from his daughter.

Danni looked mildly disappointed, but seemed to understand that there was no reason to hold onto a salt-encrusted flier.

"If you find one in good shape, I see no problem with keeping it if you want. It would look great in your scrapbook."

To this, Danni smiled and nodded. "I'm going to put a lot of stuff from this trip in the scrapbook." She'd started a scrapbook a year ago to document family trips and other exciting outings they had together, from trips as grand as a stay at the Circus Oasis to seeing a movie in the theater.

As they left the wretched little town of Bombay Beach and headed to the shore, Mica looked back at the sad mobile homes and wondered what kind of circumstances caused someone to live in such a place. Destitution, surely, or perhaps losing a job and unable to find another. Unable to pay the crazy rent in Southern California. Unable to provide for their families.

Just before turning from the little mobile home park of desolation, Mica caught a glimpse of movement from one of the windows: parted blinds shifting back into place. Then another. Watching the gawkers.

Chapter Six

G rammy Val closed her splayed fingers and pulled them from the blinds. "Goddamn nosey people."

Valerie Lazar was a tall woman with a perennial grimace on her face and an edge to her that was so hard she could just about crack a mirror with a glance. Her broad shoulders gave her a manly stature that she had always thought made her fill out a ringmaster's costume quite nicely. No one fucked with Valerie Lazar.

Francis was seated in his favorite easy chair—the arms smooth in a slick of grime; holes crudely patched with duct tape—in the corner of the room where he had a smashing good view of the television, which was one of his great pleasures in life since the cancer. He became winded easily, so he was well adjusted to his position in the chair. Sometimes just listening to his wife Valerie was exhausting enough to make him feel like he'd been walking around in the wretched heat. He had always been a spindly man who couldn't put on weight if he drank protein and carb shakes with every meal. Now, with his body struggling to fight off the sickness, he was downright skeletal and frail. The skin on his face was so thin and tight that the contours of his skull were clearly accentuated, thin wisps of white hair lying flat on his head like so many strands of cotton fiber.

Valerie crossed to the room and into the kitchen where she stirred the contents of a large pot. The air was fragrant with onions and garlic and spices. She tapped the wooden spoon on the edge of the pot and set it on the counter before putting a lid on the simmering ingredients.

"There's going to be more of that," Valerie said. "The hotel is going to bring all kinds of looky-loos. Poking around. I told Edgar it was a bad idea reopening. Goddamn waste of money, but no, he don't listen to his momma. Gotta make his own mistakes I guess."

Elric sat on a worn leather couch that didn't match Francis' chair by a decade or so. He rolled a cigarette from a crumpled package of Bugler and placed it between his lips. Tobacco hung out of the end like twisted insect legs that curled from the Bic flame he applied to it. He pulled in a deep lungful of smoke and exhaled a massive cloud. He licked his lips as if tasting the freshly burned tobacco and leaned back in the couch. "Him and Tracy are gonna do what they're gonna do."

Valerie rummaged through things in the kitchen as if the sounds of disarray were soothing to her. "Don't know what's so wrong with the way things were. We make enough to get by. Hell, more than enough, what with the shows and all. Do good with barter, too." She stepped out of the kitchen, wiping her hands on an apron that said: I Eat Vegans. "You know what Edgar put into that place? Do you?"

Elric puffed his smoke and shook his head, his beady eyes trained on his mother. His trimmed goatee and short, spiky black hair made him look far more distinguished than he was or ever could be.

"I don't know either," Valerie continued, "but I know it's a lot. All their savings. Can you believe that? I don't have no goddamned savings, and if I did I wouldn't waste it like that."

"Not just savings, ma. Investors, too. It's nice. Have you gone over there yet?"

Valerie's face tightened up. "No, and I'm not going to." She grimaced as if in disgust. "Can't believe you took a job over there."

Elric shrugged. "Gotta make that hustle, right? Eve's working there too, you know."

"I do." An evil grin etched across Valerie's face. "I think she's planning something. She has no intention on giving up the show. It's in her blood." Valerie's eyes locked on her son's. "Yours too."

Elric leaned forward and stubbed out his cigarette in an ashtray. He nodded. "Probably good to have some eyes in the hotel anyway, but there's nothing wrong with Edgar and Tracy being successful. Brings more people out here. That means more eyes on *our* show."

A grumble roiled out of Valerie's throat. "Might not be such a good thing. Too many people and they get nosey."

Francis cleared his throat. Was he clearing phlegm or attempting to gain the room's attention? Both his wife and son, figuring the latter, swiveled their heads toward the old, dying man.

Francis licked his lips as if priming them for speech. "It's a good thing Edgar is doing. We should be supporting him." His voice was raspy with age.

Valerie groaned. She regarded her husband with something like pity draped in scorn.

"You used to love the circus," Frances said as his pale brown eyes stared into his wife's dark abysmal stare. "You were the best. You . . . you could be again—"

"Bullshit!" Valerie snapped. If she could bite heads off, she would have decapitated her husband with words a long time ago. "No one wants a goddamned circus anymore. They run us out thirty years ago, and they'll do it again. We managed to weather *that* storm, but Edgar's gonna lose everything. I'm not letting him bring me down. I'll stick with what I know. People want to watch a car wreck. People want something strange and unusual. Not this hokey circus shit."

Francis wheezed. "But—"

"Don't but me, old man. I know what I'm talking about." She pried open a space in the middle of the blinds with a pair of tobacco-stained fingers. The couple and their daughter were gone. In a low voice, almost shamed, she said, "I've still got it, you know."

Eyes scanning the still, sad neighborhood, Valerie opened her mouth as if to say something else, but she saw something outside and the words caught in her throat. Her fingers splayed the blinds even more for a better view. She leaned in, eyes narrowing.

This alerted Elric, who sat up in the couch. "What is it, ma?"

Valerie blinked several times and then let out the breath she wasn't aware that she'd held in. She shook her head and then let the blinds slide shut. "Nothing."

Quiet, Valerie returned to her cooking. For a moment there she thought she saw Rascal splashing around in a stagnant pool of water in the lot next door. That was ridiculous, of course, since Grammy Val killed that dog years ago.

Chapter Seven

That evening the Burkheads retreated to their room after eating in the Oasis restaurant. The food was okay, but nothing to get excited about. Erin could tell that Mica was more focused on choosing the cheapest meal than splurging on what he really wanted, which was no splurge at all since most of the prices were only two or three dollars in difference after you eliminated the steak and seafood dishes. He went as far as suggesting certain meals to Erin. "The homestyle turkey and gravy looks good, or even a burger. Can't go wrong with a burger." Erin had her heart set on a steak, which she ordered. If Mica was going to pinch pennies, he should have ordered himself a side salad or bowl of soup.

During dinner, Erin had been kind of agitated with her husband's cheapness. He never used to be this way. In the past, she had always been the one stressing over finances, but as of late, Mica was becoming quite a cheap-ass. She had been apprehensive about the trip, the cost of gasoline, the meals. Mica had convinced her to forget about their problems, forget about the real world for just a weekend, and here he was, Mr. Hypocrite. It wasn't like she wanted him to walk on eggshells, but the tension was getting thick.

Erin set her fork down and sat back, arms crossed. "What's wrong, Mica?"

Mica finished chewing a bite of hamburger, shaking his head. "No problem. What's up?"

Eyebrows raised. "What's up? Really? You tell me."

Mica's eyes rolled toward Danni, who was eating chicken fingers and fries and more absorbed in the décor—old circus posters and memorabilia—than what her parents were talking about.

Leaning in with his arms crossed upon the table, Mica said, "I thought we could come out here and forget, just for a few days, but . . ." He shook his head, looked away, and then his eyes bore into Erin's. "It's worse than I let on, but I'm getting things under control." He said that second part quickly, before she had a chance to cut him off.

Mica knew Erin well enough to know that the look she gave him now was one of great scorn. He had ruined dinner, perhaps the entire trip. He hadn't wanted to drop the bomb on her, but there was no way to hide it. His betrayal had been eating at him. Mica thought the trip would be just what he needed to find a bit of peace, recharge his batteries and go back home with the confidence to make things right.

Erin sat back and crossed her arms. "Tell me, Mica Burkhead, just how much worse things are."

Danni was still marveling at the décor, but Mica had an idea that her ears were at least half tuned into her parents after the change in tone their conversation took.

Mica looked at his burger, but he'd lost his appetite. "It's been hard job searching. There just aren't any good positions open right now. I look everyday."

"But . . ." Erin's face twisted up. "What about the side jobs? You said you were taking on some small stuff."

"There's a lot of work out there, but the crews are full. I can't find a position I'm qualified for."

"Qualified for?" Erin's brow wrinkled. "What do you mean qualified for?"

"There haven't been any foreman positions available since I was let go."

"Wait a minute." Erin tilted her head (another gesture Mica was familiar with, that indicated her growing ire). "You told me you were making ends meet doing small jobs, picking up work on crews doing small stuff. I knew that meant you were taking a cut in pay, but you gotta do what you gotta do, right?" Mica couldn't look his wife in the eyes. "Right?"

After a lengthy sigh expelled through his nose, Mica said, "How could I take a pay cut like that? How could I go to a job site and take orders from the kind of clown I used to boss around? I couldn't do that."

"Oh really? Too much of a bruise to your fragile ego? Better to lie to your wife and—"

"I never lied to you."

"Bullshit you didn't. What the hell were you doing everyday when you left in the morning?"

Another look away in shame. "Starbucks."

"Starbucks!" Erin's voice raised an octave.

"Job hunting—"

"My ass! And I bet you were buying a coffee everyday, too. Jesus, Mica. Here I've been shopping at three different stores to get the best deals and going to the food line every week just to make ends meet, and you've been sitting in a goddamned coffee shop everyday sipping on five-dollar coffee. No wonder we're in such bad shape."

"It's not five dollars—"

"I don't care what it is. I remember you telling me once that you would do anything to keep food on the table. You said you would sling burgers if you had to. What happened to that, Mica?"

"There's food on the table."

"Barely. Because of me getting a job, and that's fine. I have no qualms over working, but I am not going to support a man who lies to his family."

Mica reached across the table and gently grabbed his wife's hand. She pulled away and then hesitated before allowing him to clutch her hand in his. "I look for work daily, that's no lie. Yes, my ego has gotten in the way. I feel like if I take a lesser position I'm going to have to work my way back up. It feels like a demotion."

"Your family should come first, before your ego. The reason you haven't been able to find work is because you're looking for the same position you had. You could have been working a long time ago, I mean, I thought you were, but . . ."

"There's something else I haven't told you." Mica tightened his grip on Erin's hand. She swallowed hard, but remained silent. "You've been telling me to try and get a government or city job, right?"

Erin nodded. "Or union."

"Right. Or union. Well, I've applied for all of those. They're not easy to get. A lot of guys are on the list. There are only so many foremen."

"Well, you have to take anything they offer you and work your way up. Have they made any offers yet?"

Mica shook his head. "I haven't said anything to you because there hasn't been any good news. I figured if I was offered one of those jobs, I would surprise you. Sitting in the coffee shop day after day I got to thinking about your stance on my career and how hardheaded I've been. I still don't like the idea of working for a union or government crew, but I understand that the benefits are really good. I haven't taken any of the small stuff also because I want to be open when one of the union jobs calls."

"Can't wait forever. I suppose you've dipped into our savings."

"Just a little."

Erin sighed, pulled her hand away. "You need to lose your pride, Mica. Seriously. When we get back you take something, anything, and you start working. If you get a call from a union job or something for the city opens up, you check that out. But you can't just sit around waiting for the best opportunity. Do that and you're going to lose everything."

Mica nodded. "I know. I didn't think things were going to be this difficult."

Erin returned to her steak, cutting a succulent morsel. Mica grabbed his burger and took a bite.

Danni looked at her parents with wide, questioning eyes. "Is everything all right?"

Mica and Erin shared a knowing glance. This weekend was supposed to be about their daughter, a celebration for her birthday, and here they were arguing about finances and money. Always money.

Erin nodded and offered her little girl an assuring smile. "Everything is going to be fine, honey. Sometimes we have to talk about adult things. Sometimes it can't be avoided no matter how much we try."

Returning the smile and then giving one to her father, Danni continued eating her chicken fingers, but soon enough she grew tired of them and pushed her plate back, indicating that she was finished eating.

"Are you full?" Mica asked.

Face scrunched up in a rictus, Danni said, "I'm not feeling so good. My tummy hurts."

After paying the bill, the Burkheads took an elevator up to their room. The steel box hummed as it lifted them up several flights. Wooziness filled Danni's guts. Typically, she would have enjoyed the slight rush, the feeling of weightlessness, but on this night she felt as if she could release her dinner at any moment.

The elevator doors opened. Standing there waiting to take the steel box down was Bette De Anza, dressed in a pair of slacks shorts, a bright flower print blouse, and sandals that showed off bright blue painted toenails. At sight of the Burkheads Bette perked up. "We just can't stop running into one another, can we?"

Erin stepped out of the elevator, followed by Mica and Danni. She said, "We just had dinner and it seems Danni's come down with something."

Bette's face soured. She knelt before Danni. "You're not feeling well, honey?"

Danni shook her head, her eyes darting downward. "I like your toenails."

"Oh, well, I wouldn't be caught dead with my nails unpainted. How do you like the color? Too much?"

Danni shook her head. "I like it."

The elevator door began to close, and Bette reached out with a hand to stop it. "I hope you feel better by tomorrow night for the Big Top Show."

Danni looked up at Bette, eyes big and full of worry. "I'm not missing the Big Top Show for anything."

Bette stepped into the elevator. "I'm sure you'll be fit as a fiddle by tomorrow, and don't ask what a fit fiddle is, 'cause I couldn't tell you."

Danni offered the woman a weak smile and waved goodbye.

"C'mon, sweetie," Erin said, chiding her daughter.

Danni watched as the elevator doors closed. Just before they connected, Danni's eyes popped wide. For a split second, a mere fraction of a moment before the doors met and the elevator was engaged, she saw something crowding Bette's feet. Something small and furry.

Dogs.

A wave of nausea swept over young Danni, causing her to waver. Her father saw this and leapt for his daughter to catch her before she spilled onto the elaborately patterned hallway carpet.

Once in the hotel room, Danni was put into bed with a cup of iced 7up (something Erin always gave her when she was sick—a tradition passed along from her own childhood). After an hour or so, Danni migrated to a chair that was placed in front of the window that overlooked the circus tent where tomorrow's Big Top Show was going to be held. Danni sat in the chair sipping 7up and looking out at the tent longingly, as if she could see the possibility of one of her great dreams passing her by.

The bubbly beverage seemed to help her stomach, but Danni still felt crummy. Her mother kept asking if this hurt and if that hurt and if she had a sore throat and did her head hurt. It was enough already. She felt better sitting there looking out the window at the circus tent (at least she told herself that). She would regret it forever if she wasn't well enough to see the show tomorrow night. Danni wasn't really sure how far they traveled to get there, but it sure seemed like quite a distance. And all for her birthday.

Swiveling her head from the constant gaze out the window, Danni looked upon her parents, lying together in one of the beds, watching television. There was a serious rift during dinner, but they seemed to have gotten over the worst of it. At least Danni hoped so. She loved her parents. They had always been very kind and gentle and loving, and when she found out they were taking her to a circus, she was over the moon. Ever since watching Dumbo when she was four, she wanted to go to a circus. When given the opportunity to redecorate her room she didn't want the typical pink and purple ponies and fairies and pixies and hearts many other girls liked. She wanted stripes on the walls, and plenty of circus animals, even a clown or two, for Danni wasn't one of those kids who were frightened of clowns. Mica painted the stripes (Danni learned a few choice four-letter words during his effort), and she and her mother went to every thrift store in town for appropriate pictures and decorations.

Danni's mother gave her a smile, one Danni recognized and cherished. In that reassuring smile everything seemed all right, even if only for a fleeting moment. Danni returned her gaze to the circus tent outside. Everything had culminated to this grand weekend. She wasn't expecting gifts or even a cake (though that *would* be nice), just a real to life circus. She wasn't even upset that the animals weren't real. If she was sick tomorrow and missed the show, her birthday would be ruined.

Danni took in a deep breath and let out a lengthy sigh. So close and yet so far.

Down below, at the entrance to the circus tent, a woman walked out. She paused and looked up at the hotel. Her blonde hair had slashes of blue and red and green. Though Danni thought the woman's hair was cool, something about her sent Danni on edge and made her stomach feel even worse than it already did.

The woman's longing gaze upward was steely and cold, and Danni could swear she looked up right into her eyes. The eyes had so much black makeup that they looked like the hollows of a skull.

Danni shivered. Her gorge rose, but she swallowed and kept the urge to vomit from taking her away from the window. It was as if she couldn't take her eyes off the woman. The sound of the television turned into a buzzing din in the background. From the entrance to the circus tent, a lion trotted out on massive paws. A feeling like vertigo washed over Danni, and she felt her head drop to her toes. The woman with the colorful hair didn't seem to notice the animal.

Danni gasped. She was only vaguely aware that her father had said something to her, for she couldn't take her eyes off what she saw below.

The woman turned away from the lion and walked, at which moment the lion opened its jaws, displaying a salivating array of gleaming teeth, and leapt. Danni yelped and closed her eyes, but only for a moment before opening them again, expecting carnage, afraid that she would see a woman being mauled by an animal Danni found to be majestic and beautiful. But no, the woman with the color-streaked blonde hair was walking away.

And there was no lion below.

Chapter Eight

Now that the Circus Oasis was opening and the Salton Sea was beginning to return to what it once was, there were signs of construction everywhere. Just up the road, a building that once housed a bowling alley was under construction, just a skeletal structure with no identity. Further down the road was a small strip mall that had somehow survived all these years, though not all of the businesses remained. The liquor store had a sign that looked very seventies and needed to be updated. A little market next door already upgraded to a gleaming new sign advertising boat rentals. Just what Bette was looking for.

After exchanging money with the clerk (and making a deal, considering she would only have until dusk, which was about an hour away), Bette found herself at the water's edge out back behind the strip mall where a line of brand-new outboard motorboats and paddle boats were docked against a virtually unblemished dock. A young family was pulling a boat in just as Bette got into number three. They had fishing poles, she noticed.

"Catch anything?" Bette asked.

The man who she assumed was the children's father beamed.

"Oh yeah! Caught a bunch." He opened a red and white Igloo cooler and lifted a small chain with five fish dangling. "Tilapia."

"I caught two of those!" the young boy on the edge of the dock said.

"That's right." the man proudly smiled. "My boy here's a natural."

Bette nodded. "Nice size, too."

The man regarded the fish like a prize before placing them back into the cooler. "Yep. I just hope there's enough room in the little freezer in the fridge in our room over there at that clown hotel. These will make a great dinner when we get home."

"Those are good looking fish. I'm glad after all these years that the Salton Sea is a place where people can do things like fish and play water sports again. Did you see anything unusual out there? Fish floating on the surface? Algae blooms?"

The man scrunched up his face. "Algae blooms?"

Bette nodded. "You'd know it if you saw it. Used to be a big problem out here. I'm studying the lake for a little while for a private research group. Seeing healthy tilapia like those ones you have there, that's the kind of thing I like."

The man shook his head. "Nope. Nothing I would consider unusual."

Bette followed the instructions taped to the outboard motor and it sang to life. She was thankful it started with a key rather than a pull cord. Bette wasn't frail; however, her experience with pull cords was one of sore shoulders and frustration. As she took off, she waved to the family and they waved back.

There's something freeing about being on the open water in a motorboat, the sound of the engine like a drone to focus one's thoughts or allow one's mind to think freely. In those moments, Bette wasn't thinking about the tilapia and the birds of the Salton Sea.

She thought about the diagnosis.

These days a cancer diagnosis wasn't the end of the world news it once was. Not always, at least. No matter, it was earth-shattering news and, in Bette's case, completely by surprise. It was a routine check up with blood work that came back a little concerning. A few more tests, some sleepless nights and boom: cancer. The doctors told her it was in the very early stages, and that was a good thing. Not to worry, Mrs. De Anza, maybe you won't even need chemo.

That one word 'maybe' ran through Bette's mind for days after the diagnosis. It haunted her dreams and darkened her waking hours. There wasn't much promise in such a word. As a child, when she would ask her mother if she could go to a movie or do something special over the weekend and her mother said 'maybe' that was a thinly veiled 'no'. Bette did the same with her own children when they were young. Maybe left it open for a possibility, which ultimately held the children at bay when the real answer was almost always no. Better handing out a maybe than hearing them whine and moan about the fact that they weren't going to go to the roller rink or the mall.

Even now, with the warm wind in her face, the salty smell of the water in her nose, and the hum of the outboard engine, *maybe* ran laps in Bette's mind. Maybe she would be okay. Maybe she *wouldn't* have to do chemo. Maybe the cancer was a false positive and she was as healthy as she felt.

Maybe she could have told Dennis.

That was the big one that troubled Bette. The trip had been planned months in advance. Dennis had no interest in spending several days in the desert, and he certainly didn't want to stay in a circus-themed hotel. He was a kind and gentle man who preferred a day on the lake under the cool shade of so many pine trees over sweating his way through a sweltering day around a lake that smelled like dead fish. Bette had told him that the lake had been cleaned up, but she knew chiding Dennis to spend time in the desert was like pulling teeth. "Maybe I'll come along," he'd said and winked that knowing wink, the one that said: hey, you know what's up, honey. You know what maybe means. Have a good time out there in the sun. Soak it up for me, babe.

Maybe.

Maybe I don't really have cancer.

Maybe it will . . . just go away.

Maybe I won't need chemo.

Bette slowed the engine. She was becoming too caught up in her own thoughts. They cascaded upon her like a tidal wave of repressed memory that threatened to push her overboard where the salty waters could pull her under and snuff them out. Over the past week, she had come to terms with her diagnosis, but she hadn't told Dennis, and that was eating her alive.

Once Bette cut the motor the boat sailed forward with the remnants of velocity, smoothly cutting through the water. The air seemed warmer now, and there wasn't a sound aside from the random fish that leapt out of the water's surface and the bird that swooped down for a bite. Bette decided to forget about the diagnosis and focus on her work. Nothing was going to change, and she would tell Dennis the news when she returned home. It would be easier to tell him now that she had some time to think. And she was sure he would understand why she waited. If Dennis was anything at all, he was an understanding man, which was rare in Bette's experience.

Floating on the placid waters, Bette wondered exactly what she had come out there for. What was she to surmise from a little boat in the middle of a huge lake? There were no fish floating by, no algae blooms sucking all the oxygen from the water. Aside from the faint odor of decay, the lake appeared as normal as any other. Given a few more months and an extensive ad campaign this place would be flourishing with jet skis and boats. Bette wasn't sure if that was such a good thing, considering the potential pollution caused by such watercrafts. Sometimes it seemed that one environmental improvement begot another environmental danger. But someone, somewhere was always making money.

After realizing that she had gone out there for no other reason than to have a moment alone with nature to think, Bette decided it was a good idea to head back. It would be difficult to get lost on a lake such as this, unlike something miles long like Lake Meade. Even so, Bette didn't want to be on the water after dark.

With the motor cranked, she turned the little boat around and cut through the still waters on her way back to the dock. Halfway back the warm whipping wind caught her floppy hat and pulled it right off her head. Bette looked back just in time to see the hat land in the roiling wake she created. At this she spun the wheel and made a decent arc, turning the boat, cautious of anyone else who might be in the lake. There was no one else. Dusk fell heavily as the sun dove behind the mountains on the western horizon. The hat in question had been with Bette for many travels around the world. She'd had a few close calls, but always managed to get it back.

She cut the motor and allowed the boat to drift toward her floating hat. She reached over the edge, arm extended, fingers splayed. She'd done this before in the Gulf of Mexico, only that time a gaffing hook was used to retrieve the hat. As the boat drifted something beneath the water's surface caught Bette's attention away from her hat and her thoughts. What she initially thought was the glimmer of scales was but a flash of white, and then another, like something beneath the water was fighting for purchase and she was getting but a glimpse through the murky depths. Bette looked closer, pulling her hand back the way a child does when she thinks a monster is under the bed. But Bette didn't stop looking. The flashes happened again, dull and white, and then she squinted when she realized that she was looking at fish bones.

But they weren't floating like they should have been.

Then she saw it again, and again.

They appeared to be swimming.

The boat shifted, and she was out of the shadow it made over the water. In the last rays of daylight, she could see a school of fish only they were composed of bone, tail fins gently swaying, connected to the spine off which branched the slender bones of their rib cages, and then the pale heads and empty eyes.

It had to be an illusion, a trick of the light. That's what Bette told herself as she watched this macabre school of fish swim away. She could hear Dennis in her mind: "You've been in the sun too long, Bette De Anza." He would most certainly use her full name, as he did on rare occasions to be explicit in a most playful way.

She closed her eyes, felt the gentle sway of the boat, and took in several deep breaths. She had expected to see dead fish in the Salton Sea. She had expected it, and so that's what her weary mind showed her. She just didn't expect to see them swimming around.

Bette opened her eyes. The hat was within reach, so she stretched out her arm and grabbed it after a moment's hesitation. When she pulled it away, she felt a tug as if the hat had been caught on something. There was movement. It happened so fast that she couldn't believe her eyes as she stared at the circular ripples that spread from the place where her hat had been. She stared, eyes wide, tremors of fear crawling through her body like so many ants crawling beneath her skin. Her head shook like something palsied. The hat now lay on the floor of the boat, soggy in a small pool of lake water.

Bette couldn't take her eyes off of that spot where the ripples had dissipated, and a placid sheen took their place.

She couldn't take her eyes off of the spot where she had seen the giraffe's head.

Part Two

Friday

By the time Katherine made it to the area in the desert that felt right, the sun had come up. The warmth was something she didn't yearn for, knowing that the walk back to her tent in Slab City would be an excruciating one.

This box of tramp art was intricately carved with an arc-load of animals that all blended together in an almost psychedelic motif. The detail was so intricate it must have taken the artist a lifetime and a steady hand to carve. Katherine set the box on the surface of the sand. It wasn't a place she made a conscious decision about, but something she felt within, something harbored in her soul for the many years she had roamed the earth a tortured soul. She did not know or understand the meaning of the boxes or why she was compelled to travel on foot to disperse them. She hardly made it back to Slab City from the Salton Sea when she deposited the first box yesterday morning. The way she felt now, the exhaustion, the morning heat from a rising sun, she was sure this would be the last box.

The sand around the intricate piece of art shifted, and then roiled like something alive. The box began to sink like in a pool of quicksand in an old cartoon. Once the little cube of art was gone, Katherine felt a surge within her body that caused an incredible flash of shivers. Gooseflesh raised the hairs on her arms. The sunburned woman collapsed onto the desert floor.

Minutes later she felt something lapping at her face. It was a familiar feeling, one any dog lover is well acquainted with.

"Rascal?" Her voice was faint, dreamy.

Eyes shot open. The warm licking stopped. Katherine used the back of her hand to feel her cheek, but there was no residual moisture from an eager dog's lapping tongue.

Rascal.

Chapter Nine

The following morning Danni woke up before her parents, and her first thought was that there was just one more day until the Big Top Show. She sat up in bed, relieved that the nausea from last night was gone. Her empty stomach gurgled for sustenance. This was a good sign that her sickness had been what her mother called the twenty-four-hour flu. Danni thought that was a funny name since those little flus didn't really last a full twenty-four hours.

She pivoted to see the shapes of her parents beneath the sheets, her father's meaty leg free of the covers and probably as chilled as a side of beef, considering the air conditioner that blew directly on that particular appendage. His snoring was a rough and inconsistent Harley idle. It was amazing her mother could get any sleep next to that man. It was amazing that Danni managed to sleep in the same room with him.

Danni crept out of the warmth of her bed and eased over to the chair she had left beside the window. Her parents must have drawn the heavy curtains before they went to sleep last night. They were those ultra-thick curtains that were three deep, typical for a hotel to blot out absolutely every ray of morning sunlight.

Danni grabbed the corner of said curtains and gently pushed the thick folds of fabric aside. The ray of sunshine that breached the room was like a beam of fire threatening to wake her parents with its mere presence.

Peaking out of the sliver of window that she dared reveal for fear of bringing way too much light into the room, Danni almost expected to see the lion again, staring up at her. But no. The big top tent was bright in the morning sun, strips of red and white like a giant piece of stretched candy cane. The flags at its points whipped in the wind. An elderly couple in clothes fit for a safari walked the tent's perimeter, pointing and smiling, probably reliving old memories of circuses past. Danni smiled watching them. They looked so happy. It was good to see her parents look at each other like that, but lately those moments were fleeting. Danni tried not to think about the big "D" word, but it was an evil reality that nagged at her mind, especially when her mother and father were in the midst of one of their more raucous arguments. They weren't violent or anything, just loud. Through the tears and covering her ears, Danni didn't really know what they fought about, what was so important to a couple of people who supposedly loved one another. What could be so bad? What, in their lives together, was awful enough to yell at one another loud enough to bother the neighbors? Danni couldn't understand this.

But tomorrow night was the big night. The Big Top Show. Danni had been looking forward to this for a long time, ever since her parents surprised her with the wonderful birthday gift of this weekend trip. Hopefully, they could keep their emotions in check and not ruin her time. Danni was perceptive enough to see that things had teetered here and there. It was so bad at times she felt as if she were treading thin ice, watching what she said, what she asked of them. Thoughts that perhaps she had done something to cause the rift between her parents tormented her at times. During the ride to the Salton Sea she felt guilty, as if it was her fault they were making the trip. This was for her birthday, after all. Maybe if they hadn't come out here her parents would be getting along better.

"How are you feeling?" The voice was but a whisper fighting for purchase against a roaring snore factory.

Danni pulled her gaze away from the tent outside and her mind from the same thoughts that troubled her when she found it difficult to fall asleep at night. She offered a big smile, always concealing those deep thoughts of potential divorce and which parent she would choose to live with were she forced to (her friend Chloe had to go through such an ordeal, and though the girl made it sound positive to be getting twice as many gifts at Christmas and her birthday, Danni didn't like the idea of her parents splitting up).

Danni nodded. "I'm feeling much better." She thought, *she's gonna say it, she's gonnna say it!*

"Must have been a twenty-four-hour bug."

She said it! Danni giggled inwardly, which must have shown in her face,

"You look excited."

Nodding her head, Danni said, "I can't *wait* for the circus show."

Mica's snoring stuttered a moment as if he was choking on his larynx, which caused Danni to hold in a breath, as if her exclamation had been too boisterous and threatened to wake him. His snoring returned to its inconsistent and yet somehow consistent stammer, and Danni couldn't help but giggle, covering her mouth with her hand as not to wake her father. She found his weird snoring to be a fairly hilarious, constantly amused when he fell asleep on the couch and really got going. She didn't understand sleep apnea, and he was in denial that there was a problem.

"Well, I'm glad you're excited, and I'm glad you're feeling better."

Erin sat up and removed herself from the sheets, yawning and stretching as she sauntered between the beds and toward the bathroom. She said, over her shoulder, "You can put on some cartoons if you want. Your father isn't going to wake up that easy."

"Okay." But Danni had no intention of watching cartoons. She looked outside, watching the tent and hoping for that lion again. Had it been some kind of vision? Something brought on by a fever?

That's what her parents told her. She had been apprehensive about confessing what she had seen, but it was so weird and unusual that she had to. They had been worried about it and checked her temperature, but she had none. That's when they suggested that she lay down and try to sleep.

The lion seemed so real. The image in her mind seemed so real.

After Mica woke up and Danni suggested room service for breakfast, a suggestion she quickly regretted after seeing the anguish in her father's eyes and the tension increase in the room tenfold, they settled on seeing what the continental breakfast included.

Along a wall flanking the lobby were two long buffet tables with an array of typical continental breakfast fare. Cereal, fruit, granola bars, cups of yogurt, loaves of bread and a toaster, chilled pitchers of milk and orange juice. It wasn't exactly what Danni was expecting after being told a continental breakfast was like a buffet, but she could settle for some toast and yogurt if it kept the peace.

After gathering up a sufficient breakfast and idle banter with other guests, they retreated to their room to eat and plan the rest of the day. For Danni, there wasn't much to plan. All she cared about was the Big Top Show, and after talk that maybe she had suffered from heat stroke yesterday rather than some twenty-four-hour flu, she had no real intention to go out in the sun for fear of a repeat that would ruin the rest of the trip.

"I got an idea," Mica said between bites on a mealy apple. "We could go check out that Salvation Mountain place."

Erin shrugged, scrunching her face up like she didn't really like the idea but wasn't going to express those feelings just yet. "Maybe we can rent a boat and go out on the water. There's got to be a place that rents out little motorboats."

Mica nodded, though there was no enthusiasm in the gesture. He glanced at Danni. "What about the birthday girl? What would you like to do?"

Danni sat in her bed with her back to the wall fidgeting with a set of magnets that looked like obsidian rocks. When they were stuck together they formed a bracelet that fit around Danni's wrist. She liked to play with them, testing the positive and negative force. She liked that she could use the negative end of one magnet and push another across a table without touching them together.

"All I want to do is go to the Big Top Show."

Her mother offered a sympathetic look. "Well, okay, honey, but there's a lot of time in the day for other things. Is there anything else you can think of that you would like to do?"

A shrug of indifference. A tilt of the head. "I just don't want to do anything else, that's all." She smiled with big clear eyes, overdoing it a bit. "Why don't we stay in the hotel today and watch a movie or something?"

Mica grimaced, confused. "We can watch movies any day of the week, sweetie. Let's go outside and do something fun. Doesn't Salvation Mountain sound like fun?" Erin shot him a coy glance of venom that Mica caught. "Or a boat ride would be great too. Don't you think?"

Danni didn't want to tell her parents that she didn't want to go out in the sun. She didn't want to do anything that would jeopardize seeing the Big Top Show. Her sudden burst of cheerfulness at staying in the hotel fizzled out. She hung her head as if she had done something wrong.

"Oh, I think I know what's up," Erin said. Danni looked up as if she had been caught doing something she shouldn't have been. Erin just nodded her head, that slight hint of a smile playing upon her lips like she did when she caught onto something. "You're afraid to go back out in the sun. Think you're going to get heatstroke again, if that's what you *had*."

There was no use hiding it. Danni just nodded her head, tightlipped.

Erin sat on the bed beside her daughter and put an arm around the little girl. "We don't know that you suffered from heatstroke yesterday. We don't really know at all what happened. But you can't live your life being afraid."

The little girl's voice was but a delicate piece of hand-blown glass. "I just don't want to miss the show."

Looking over her daughter's head, Erin and Mica shared one of those looks parents give each other when faced with little decisions that rarely came up, such as this one. It was a look that said, well, what are we going to do about this. For the most part they agreed on discipline, which had always been pretty easy considering that Danni had been an easy kid (just wait until puberty!). The question at hand was whether they succumb to Danni's wishes to stay in the hotel or continue to encourage her to go outside.

Finally, after a silence that seemed to alter time, Danni said, "I'd like to go on the boat ride tomorrow if that's okay." Her voice had a pleading tone to it that was always a bit of a heartbreaker coming from a child who was so sweet.

Mica stood from the bed where he had been sitting on the edge and walked to the stationary table where a little container with a plastic liner held ice cubes in a pool of cold water. He scooped a couple of cubes into a little plastic cup and poured cola over them. "I have an idea."

Chapter Ten

The idea of being cooped up in the hotel room all day didn't sit well with Erin and Mica. After careful consideration, they decided that it was a good opportunity to give their daughter some responsibility. On a few occasions Erin had left Danni home alone for maybe twenty minutes when Mica was at work and she had to run to the store. She'd had that fear of what would happen were she to get into a car accident. How would Danni respond when her mother was late getting back? How long before emergency personnel called? There was a certain instinct to coddle Danni, to protect her at all costs (people called that being helicopter parents), but Erin and Mica knew they had to give their little girl some rope. She was old enough for a little bit of responsibility. Erin left Danni with her phone and strict instructions not to open the door for anyone (the Do Not Disturb sign was left on the door handle), not that anyone would knock.

Erin was confidant with their decision, and though Mica was the one who suggested allowing Danni some independence, he was already worried about her, and they were only as far as the lobby.

"Your phone is fully charged, right?" Mica said as they approached the doors to the parking lot.

"Sixty-five percent."

Mica stopped in the middle of the lobby. He looked worried. "You left a charger, right?"

"Sixty-five percent charge will last all day. We're going to be gone for an hour. I wouldn't worry about it."

Nodding, Mica said, "Yeah, I guess you're right." He shook his head and attempted a smile, but it wasn't genuine.

"We're just going to be an hour or so," Erin said. "It's healthy to give her this kind of space. And really, she wouldn't want to stay by herself in a hotel if it wasn't for the whole sunstroke thing. She wants to see that Big Top Show so bad she doesn't want anything to mess it up. Besides, it's her birthday. If she wants to stay in the hotel all day, that's her prerogative."

Perhaps sensing the distress between the couple, they were approached by a man in a suit who smelled heavily of mid-grade cologne like he reapplied the stuff every hour on the hour. He put a hand on one of each of their shoulders in a gesture that was a little too personal, which somehow went perfectly with the douse of cologne. Mica immediately pulled back, fearing that the smell of the guy would seep into his shirt and be stuck with him all day. The stupid grin the guy wore was car salesman worthy.

"How is your stay with us?" he asked, speaking through that absurd grin.

Caught off guard, Mica looked perturbed. He was still thinking about the cologne, hoping it wouldn't give him a headache or linger too long. He'd never trusted guys like this one. You could smell them coming a mile away and they always seemed plastic, like they had gotten where they were in life by making shady deals loaded with false promises. A bone fide bull-shitter.

Erin shrugged, which was part of her more polite way of getting the guy's greasy paw off of her shoulder. "Okay, I guess."

"Not too bad, I suppose," Mica said. He focused on the name badge. "Edgar. "Had a little issue yesterday with the desk clerk, but I guess it's not so bad, all things considered. Opening day's gotta be pretty tough on a new business." He offered a false chuckle that was a bit more condescending than he expected.

The man's domineering smile had no intent on diminishing. "Well, you see, this is actually a *re*-opening. The Circus Oasis was a popular resort and attraction in the 1970s. It's been a long time coming, but we finally managed to bring it back. If you have any questions or concerns, don't hesitate to tell us. We will do our very best to accommodate you. Consequently, after your stay if you could Yelp us and leave reviews on popular websites, we would be appreciative beyond belief. There are some critics here to see the Big Top Show for review in Southern California papers, but I think it's the reviews of the general public that matter. Are you looking forward to the Big Top Show?"

Mica's face twisted up a bit. "Uh, yeah, well, you see, we came here for our daughter. She's an animal lover, so we thought this would be a great surprise for her birthday."

The man's madcap grin finally slipped into an expression of exaggerated confusion. Had he half a chance, he could have been a hell of a character actor back in the Laurel and Hardy days. Maybe in silent films.

"Daughter?"

"She's up in our room," Erin said. "Danni wasn't feeling well last night."

Edgar switched his expressive face to that of shock. "Is she all right?"

"She's fine. But she doesn't want to go out. Thinks the sun is what made her feel crummy last night. She's *really* looking forward to the show tonight." Her lips tightened in a way that almost required sympathy.

The supercharged smile was back. "Well, that's good." Edgar paused, but not for long. Clearly, he didn't favor even a breath of silence. "Heading out on the water? They rent boats and jet skis over at the convenience store just up the road. We will eventually do the same, but one step at a time." Now his turn for a not-so-genuine chuckle.

Mica said, "Uh, no, maybe tomorrow. We're just going out for an hour or so. Gonna check out Salvation Mountain. Looks like it might be interesting. I saw something about it on TV once. Some old nudist runs the place; paints murals on the sand dunes or something."

For the first time, Edgar's ridiculous display of joviality dropped. It was amazing how sinister he looked when he slanted his eyes. Reminded Mica of a train robber in a silent movie. Edgar swiveled his head toward the front desk in the lobby where a young woman with colorful hair stood sentinel. She looked as if she were suffering from a migraine and sucking on lemons. Edgar looked at Mica and Erin once again, less sinister, more exasperated, as if all the wild changes in expression had worn him out.

"You don't want to go messing around with some painted dunes in the desert, do you?" He shook his head. "You ask me, it's not what it's cracked up to be."

Mica nodded. "Huh. Okay," he squinted at the name tag again, "Edgar." Mica put his hand out as if to pat Edgar on the shoulder in a good-natured manner, but decided against it for fear of becoming tainted with cheap cologne. "Thanks for the tip."

Mica looked at the peculiar girl with the colorful hair behind the desk at the lobby doors. She was whispering something into the ear of the guy who wasn't very helpful yesterday when they had come into the lobby with the strange animal claw. Edgar approached them and words were exchanged. Mica couldn't hear what they were saying, but Edgar's sinister eyes were back, and he pointed in Mica and Erin's direction. The color-haired girl looked up, her eyes catching Mica's, and he looked away the way a guy does when he'd been caught admiring a beautiful woman.

Chapter Eleven

After the Burkheads left the lobby, Edgar dropped the fake smile act and turned his attention to his daughter. She had her eyes trained on him like she had been trying to seer a hole in the back of his head while he conversed with their guests. He loathed that look. It always seemed to be there. It was a teenager look that she held firmly right into her twenties. In fact, it had gotten worse over the years, that look. A grown man shouldn't allow himself to be intimidated by his daughter, but Eve had been given too much leeway all her life. Kids grew up different in trailer parks out in the middle of nowhere, especially with a family of carnies going back three generations. Edgar wanted to get away from the trashy carnie life his parents were lost in, but here he was opening up the hotel again, circus theme and all. He rationalized it as a smart business move, and with the proper care this place could turn into a destination. What with the circus animals made out of metal parts and rubber skins, there wouldn't be any of that other nonsense his mother always insisted was just "part of the job" that Edgar pretty much knew she thrived on. Problem was his daughter had become a pupil of her grandmother, whether he liked it or not, and he was beginning to see the startling signs of sadism in the young woman.

"What?" Eve said, her voice beyond snotty.

Edgar detected anger in that voice. Why? What had he done to make his daughter hate him so? He'd only been a father to her. He'd only tried to make the best for her in all these years of destitution and struggle. Why couldn't she see that this right here, right now, was the result of their struggles? There was a good life to be had, and yet she regarded him like she hated him, and that broke his heart.

Edgar pushed his feelings aside and strode across the lobby. He rounded the counter and gestured with a finger for Eve to follow him into the back. She looked at him, rolled her eyes, and sighed. "What is it?"

The way Eve talked to Edgar made him want to cry and yell in equal measure.

"Come here. I want to have a word with you."

Edgar looked into the employee space behind the front desk and hollered, "Jeff, come out for a few, please."

Jeff, a young man with a beard that failed to hide his second and third chin adequately, rushed out with a hearty, "yes, sir!" and relieved Eve at the front desk. Jeff had known the Lazar family all his life, having grown up in the trailer park, and was excited to have a real job for a change. The poor guy thought working the front desk in a fledgling revamped hotel was his big break.

Edgar, voice stern, said, "C'mon, Eve. Now." He turned and walked into the employee area, not looking back. The only way he could get his daughter to do anything he asked of her was to be an asshole, which broke his heart to no end. At this point, the love he once felt for the girl had been trampled upon and pushed away so much that he was beginning to feel more comfortable treating her like shit. She treated everyone like shit and seemed to kind of appreciate that sort of thing. It was a weird dynamic for Edgar. At this rate, Eve was going to be worse than her grandmother.

About a solid minute after Edgar left the lobby Eve followed. No too close to seem eager for whatever her father had to say.

"So, what's up, Daddy?" She offered a stupid smile that exuded sarcasm. She only called him daddy when she was in a mood, which was pretty much always. Edgar hated it. She'd stopped calling him daddy when she was a little girl, opting for "dad" until she became twice the rebellious kid in her twenties that she'd been in her teens.

"Look, I've told you before that this is a business, and I expect you to treat the customers with the utmost respect. It's a strange concept, right? Respect?"

"I treat people just fine. Treat people they way they treat me."

"Let me guess, you treat them like shit because you don't like the way they look at you."

Eve shrugged. "Well, I don't."

"Maybe if you had a smile and a friendly attitude they would greet you with a smile. Ever thought about that? I see you standing behind that desk, and you look like you want to murder someone. What the fuck is up with that? People don't want to see that first thing when they walk into the hotel they're staying at."

"What are they going to do, turn around and go back home? Not like there's any other options out here."

"That's not the point, Eve. Christ! What don't you get? You need to treat people better. You might treat your mom and me like shit, but don't you dare treat the people staying here any less than they deserve." Eve opened her mouth to say something, but Edgar cut her off. "And don't give me any of that 'I treat them the way they treat me' bullshit. I don't want to hear it."

"Whatever."

"Don't whatever me."

Eve raised her eyebrows, shook her head, and held out her hands in a "what the fuck do you want from me" gesture.

Edgar clenched his teeth, grinding the molars together like he was trying to make his gums bleed. "And another thing."

Eve let out a breath like someone had pushed on her chest hard enough to expel air directly out of her lungs. She flicked her head to dislodge an ornery lock of red and blue hair from her face, batted her eyes, and pouted her lips. "Yes, daddy?"

"You and your grandmother aren't messing around those painted mountains anymore, are you?"

Eve shrugged. "Maybe."

Edgar leaned in close. "Dammit. Part of why I worked so hard to reopen the hotel was so that we didn't need to fuck around with the little stuff." He took a breath and deflated a bit, shameful for some of the things he'd done in the past to make ends meet. The eighties were dark years for the Lazar family no matter which way you cut it. "This is our opportunity to do things on the up and up. The mountain is a thing of the past, right? 'Cause it should be. Especially if people are going to be going out there looking around."

"It's a tourist trap."

Edgar shook his head. "No, it's not. A tourist trap has gift shops, restaurants, stuff like that. It's an oddity, like the huge hot dog in LA or the world's largest thermometer in Barstow. It isn't even as well known as that. Just some naked hippie's colorful wet dream." Edgar narrowed his eyes. "You haven't been messing around out there anymore, have you? Tell me the truth."

Eve shrugged. "You and mom are the only ones who believe in this hotel. You know that, right? This isn't what Grammy remembers. Fake animals? Really? It's so stupid. It isn't going to work, so why would we stop our little business? Huh?"

Edgar realized that he'd been holding in a breath and let it out slowly through his nose. He nodded. "I suppose I get that, but you know I don't approve of what you do. Just tell me one thing. Will you give it up once you see that the hotel is profitable?"

To this, Eve smiled, but her eyes were slanted and devilish. "Do you *really* think Grammy is going to stop?"

Edgar stood there for another moment, frozen in the icy chill of his daughter's response. Grammy most certainly had that girl under her thumb. He walked away, leaving the not so faint aroma of cologne in his wake.

Eve pulled out her cell phone and dialed a number. She put the phone to her ear. "Grammy? We have a problem."

Chapter Twelve

Bette lingered in the hallway just off the front lobby, examining the walls of photographs from the first incarnation of the Circus Oasis Hotel. Some pictures were blown up and displayed in intricate frames with circus-themed detail, such as carved lions and tigers or even smiling circus clowns, and the others, most of them nine by tens or maybe twelve by sixteens, were in simple gold frames.

After what happened on the lake it took a couple of vodka and tonics to put Bette back on her feet. There was a lot of rationalizing. It must have been a fish that jumped out of the water just as she grabbed her hat and caught her by surprise. Her mind filled in the blanks with something irrational. That's what it had to be. That's what a few drinks convinced her of anyway. And those paw prints on the beach, the ones that looked like they came from a large cat . . . well, whose to say there aren't mountain lions nearby? Deep down she knew there weren't. Hell, not even deep down. She knew good and well that there were no mountain lions for miles around. They thrived in a completely different eco system. There was nothing to explain the large cat prints. Time passed, and they didn't seem as big, as threatening.

There appeared to be a chronological order to the pictures on the wall. The early ones were black and white. According to the brief caption at the bottom, they were from the Lazar Carnival Sideshow. In the picture, a group of carnies were grouped around an old-fashioned circus wagon with the family name emblazoned on it. They looked fairly miserable, like maybe the photo was taken at the end of a particularly arduous tour, or maybe in the midst of a life of touring that appeared to have no end. The next several photos were in grainy muted colors and had probably been blown up from originals. The dates were from the fifties and sixties. This generation of the Lazar family was much more cheerful. One photo was of a carnival barker standing at a podium dressed in a striped shirt colored like a barber's pole in mid shout with a crowd watching, enthralled. Another was of a curvy beauty in a shimmering gown standing in front of a large banner that said: Phantasmagoria! In another photo, a caravan of cages held tigers and lions and elephants like an image on a vintage box of animal crackers. Bette had seen cartoons when she was young that depicted animals in cages, but she had never seen photographic evidence of such barbaric behavior. These were majestic animals that deserved to be on the veldt. Seeing them like this broke her heart.

After several more photos from this era, Bette came upon the first picture of the Circus Oasis Hotel circa 1969. While the counterculture of the sixties was peaking with Kent State and the Manson murders, the Lazar family was gearing up for the most ambitious feat their many generations of carnie barkers and performers had embarked on. Beautiful shots in color and black and white of the hotel, the circus tent. And some of the performances within the tent. One of the blown-up pictures depicted a woman in a ring mistress uniform with a bullwhip, one leg sheathed in a sleek and shining boot kicked up on a wooden chair (the type typically used during a lion taming performance). She had an impeccable red and black tux with tails and a top hat. Like Joan Crawford in that old B-movie, only this sort of thing didn't happen in real life, not in the sixties. Bette was impressed.

She moved along the wall, taking in the photos with wonder and apt interest, her mind returning to the blow-up of the ring mistress who appeared in many of the other photos smiling brightly and holding her head high. Iconic images. History. Clowns, animals, jugglers, high wire walkers, and more.

A sound drew Bette's attention from the wall of photos. She looked up toward the lobby. A flash of color, yellow, orange. Someone walking up to the front counter? Wearing leopard print?

Bette rubbed her eyes. There was a headache setting in. She'd been trying to ignore it, but it was there. A feeling of unease had been enveloping her ever since the boat ride. When Bette was a little girl, she used to see things from the corner of her eye. At the time she was convinced that she saw the ghosts of her grandmother and younger brother who had been killed in a car accident, but her mother told her that she was just imagining things. As Bette got older, she remembered those glimpses, and they seemed as spiritual as ever. She figured that the older you got, the less susceptible you were to the spiritual world. She liked to think that her cat, Mr. Bigsley, could see into that other realm, but she also knew that might just be wishful thinking. Mr. Bigsley was distinguished, after all.

Returning her attention to the wall of photographs, Bette was suddenly aware of faint calliope music. In some nostalgic way, the music set her at ease. Clown pictures that might have looked menacing to a young child or an older woman were now jolly and grin worthy.

But then the photos changed.

The ring mistress continued to stand tall, but the smile had melted into a sneer. The eyes were the same. Bette didn't like those eyes. They were sinister. Her gaze drifted from the ring mistress to the lion, and then Bette's mouth gaped. The lion was skinny, its ribs showing like the bars of a xylophone. Its fur was thin, its mane disheveled. In the next picture, a clown was sad. The paint on his face was grinning, but his lips were caught in a frown. After that, Bette saw a cage with two emaciated tigers. Her eyes widened. The next picture showed the ring mistress cracking her whip at a terrified lion, its body scarred with red, inflamed pinstripes.

They're not supposed to abuse the animals.

This is sick.

The next picture depicted two sad clowns standing beside a cage with what appeared to be dead tigers. The animals' tongues protruded from gaping, toothless maws.

Bette shook her head. Who would post such atrocious pictures in a hotel, and why?

The calliope music shifted from melodic major notes to something of a minor pentatonic scale that slowly slipped into a cacophonic mess that seemed to hit weird pressure points in Bette's mind. It was like the music was pushing tender nerve endings and releasing jolts of pain that threatened a spontaneous headache.

Bette's adrenaline increased. Her eyes watered, but she was far too angry for tears. If this is what the Circus Oasis Hotel was all about, she wanted no part of it. To display such photos was egregious; it was absurd and cruel.

Then Bette saw the last photo and she gasped. The ring mistress was smiling again, those sadistic eyes gleaming like polished obsidian. Instead of one leg crooked on a chair, she had her boot up on a decapitated elephant head.

Backing away in horror, Bette couldn't take her eyes off the offensive photo, as if it would come to life and that evil woman would step into reality to cut off Bette's head and hold it up triumphantly. It couldn't possibly be legal to display such atrocious photographs. It was animal snuff. In the middle of a hotel? What about the children?

Finally turning and letting the offensive picture out of her sight, Bette stomped her way to the front desk where a young woman with wild hair stood smirking as if she could just see that this customer was disgruntled and no, she wasn't going to be of help. After those photos, Bette was in no mood for someone's bad attitude.

Eyes stern, beckoning. "I'm absolutely ap*palled* by the photos in the hallway. Especially the last one. How *dare* the Circus Oasis brazenly display such violent and gory images." Overcome with emotion and not releasing the pressure valve verbally, Bette's voice cracked, and she had to make a serious effort not to cry.

The girl behind the counter (Eve, according to the nametag) deepened her annoying smirk, her stupid shit-eating grin. She rolled her eyes, fluttering them a bit, an action of which caused Bette to roil within, and said, "What's wrong with the pictures? That's my family you're talking about."

To this, Bette took a step back in horror. Pride! There was pride in this dingbat girl's snotty response. "Slaughtered animals? That, that evil woman standing over the decapitated head of an elephant? It's sick!"

Eve wrinkled her brow in confusion and misunderstanding. She was expressive, this girl. Had a way of communicating without saying a word; however, she was more than willing to use her words in defense, or offensive speech, whichever was required of her. It was a demeanor that didn't fit with the uniform. She flung two words like darts with honed points: "Show me," to which Bette reared her head back in a manner so exaggerated that little miss expression had to have gotten the gist, the non-verbal communication Bette was laying down.

Nodding slightly. "Follow me." Bette turned and began her

walk down the hallway without looking back to see if Eve was following.

The pictures on the wall swam by in blurs of black and white and circus color for Bette was focused on that last picture, the one that made her guts clench. If these were the pictures grand enough to be displayed, then what kind of sick stuff did they keep in the family photo albums? What kind of twisted horror show photographs were kept in boxes tucked away in an attic somewhere? What kind of . . .?

Stopped in her tracks quick enough to have Eve bump into her were Eve following that close, Bette froze. She shook her head slowly at first, the way someone does when they can't believe what they are seeing. She really couldn't believe her eyes. No way. This wasn't real. This wasn't happening.

The picture was gone. In its place was the same exact shot, only this time the woman in the perfectly tailored ring mistress suit with glorious tails was standing with one leg crooked, foot firmly planted on a wooden chair, the type typically used in the ring with the ferocious lion, of which was on its haunches as if posing.

Pivoting her head to glance at Eve who stood several paces back, Bette's face said everything, her eyes drawn, complexion drained of color. As if she had seen a ghost, as the saying goes. As if something she was certain of had suddenly vanished.

"My grandma," Eve said after Bette returned her gaze to the proud photograph. "So, what's all this decapitation shit?" Eve's lips crooked up. "For a second there I thought you were going to show me something cool."

Bette's head swiveled slow like her neck was made of creamy peanut butter. The look on her face said everything, and she could tell by the look on Eve's face that the girl got off on spooking this older woman, this fragile and delicate thing who was beginning to see phantom photographs of animal cruelty.

Bette just shook her head and walked by Eve without a word. What was she going to say to the girl? She would have liked to see a decapitated elephant. It would have given her a thrill. Bette had no time for sickos like Eve.

On top of that, she was beginning to worry about her mind. First the prints in the sand, then the thing in the water, and now this? Maybe it was the sun. Maybe she was suffering from heat stroke.

She took the elevator to her room and, after filling the little bucket up with ice, she drank three little plastic cups of ice water and cranked the air conditioner. She knew it wasn't heat stroke. She didn't have symptoms. The problem was that she didn't know what was going on and why she was having these little hallucinations.

You're not cracking up, are you, Bette old girl?

Bette shook her head. Hell no. She was very in control of her mind.

That's what made the photograph in the lobby hallway so frightening.

Chapter Thirteen

The drive to Salvation Mountain was only twenty minutes from Bombay Beach, but those were twenty tense minutes for the Burkheads considering their daughter was sitting in the hotel room, probably watching TV or dreamily looking out the window at the circus big top, imagining majestic animals in a far more glorious fashion than any circus could ever provide. Danni could handle an hour alone, but it just felt wrong. They had made a collaborative decision years ago not to be helicopter parents always hovering over their daughter like they could save her from a scraped knee or the harmful taunts of her peers, but that proved to be more difficult than anticipated. Those parks and playgrounds were like combat zones. Germs, heights, bullies, weird men that *might* be someone's father and then again *might* be lingering to snatch up a kid.

She was safe in a locked hotel room. And she had Erin's phone in case of emergency. Danni was a smart girl, and both Erin and Mica did their very best not to underestimate her intelligence. They knew that for Danni this little test was enjoyable and perhaps the gateway to more independence in her future. For

Mica and Erin, it was a freefall without a parachute from their parenting helicopter.

The road to Salvation Mountain was snaked with fine golden sand on either side like the desert was making a concerted effort to admonish the road and take back her kingdom from the pesky humans who thought they could plant tracks on her wind-blown pastures.

"That's got to be it," Erin said, perking up to see something emerging in the distance.

Mica squinted behind his sunglasses. "Not as colorful as I expected. Not like what I saw on TV."

"It's still far off. Hopefully it's not a mirage." She smirked, but the joke didn't so much as crack a grin on Mica's face.

As they approached, Mica slowed the car. A cautious eyeful of rearview mirror showed him there were no cars in sight. Between the road and the mountain was what looked like some kind of weird junkyard of broken-down cars, heaping hills of paint in five gallon and single gallon buckets, a rusted tractor with at least an inch of sand on its surfaces, and several makeshift sheds that contained who knew what. Cut into a berm of rock and sand, an entryway opened into what once served as a parking lot, though there weren't any people milling about like Mica had expected. No cars that hadn't been there long enough to acquire a coat of sand.

Mica pulled into the entrance and stopped before entering the parking area between the road and the mountain. Erin read the words that were painted on the side of the mountain amongst a clustering of random images and phrases in dark and foreboding hues as opposed to the bright rainbow of delight this place once was known for. "Damnation Mountain."

Mica whispered, "Jesus."

Erin's eyes widened, mouth slightly agape. "So, this is what you brought me out here to see?"

Mica just shook his head.

The sound of an approaching car drew Mica from the trance he slipped into as they sat there half in the road, witnessing this monstrous collection of deviant art before them. A quick look over his shoulder showed him that a car was indeed traveling from the direction they had come. To avoid the possibility of being hit in the rear and throwing the car into a spin that would launch them right into damnation, he pulled into the lot and slipped in next to one of the cars that appeared to have been heaped there a good five or six years ago. The little dunes at the wheels were yet more evidence that Mother Nature was taking her land back.

Mica kept the engine running. They were silent for a spell, just looking at the painted dunes, the images of clowns and devils and knives and skulls. Phrases like *The Greatest Show in HELL* and *Gleaming and Glittering with Gold, Wonderful Surprises for Young and Old.*

"I'm not going out there," Erin said, shaking her head. "No way."

"It looks spooky, but it's just a roadside attraction. It's free to look around."

Erin gave her husband a look like he was rationalizing the maiming of a young child. "Are you fucking kidding me? This place is a tomb."

"I mean, it looks creepy as shit, but how can we not look around?" Mica whispered the next words: "It's weird."

Erin sighed, but there was some kind of allure that Mica couldn't deny. This was nothing like what he had seen on TV. The Salvation Mountain he expected was filled with religious phrases and vibrant color, rainbows and peace. This was something vomited from the roiling bowels of Satan himself.

"I'm going to have a look around." It was a statement, but Mica looked at Erin with question marks in his eyes, waiting for her affirmation.

Erin sighed. "We should go back to the hotel. This is Danni's birthday, remember?"

"But we didn't come out here for nothing. I don't want to stay long or anything. I just want to have a quick look around." Mica could see that Erin didn't like this at all. Her mouth was clenched tight like she was about to explode. He recognized this and still couldn't resist the urge to slip down this mountainous rabbit hole. "Are you coming?"

"No."

One tight syllable. She looked through the passenger side window, away from Mica, deep in thought. Ignoring him. Condemning him in restrained silence. He was in it now, and he knew it, but he *had* to look around. It would be worth talking himself out of the doghouse. They had a twenty-minute ride back to the hotel. That would probably be enough time to calm her down, especially if he didn't waste too much time exploring this place.

Leaving the engine running with the A/C blowing arctic air into the car, Mica exited and glanced at Erin once more, for one last judgment of her demeanor. It was easy to tell what mood she was in based solely on facial expression, and she was pissed. If there was such a thing as women's intuition, Mica was ignorant of it and more attracted to something shiny. He knew that Erin had called him a dumb ox under her breath, but he ignored her. That was a phrase she used a lot; one he was used to. She wouldn't cool down anytime soon, but he could deal with the fire.

The series of painted sand dunes was about as large as a sprawling estate. Stairs were notched out of the side of the dunes here and there, leading to its various levels. At the edge of the strange spectacle, Mica tapped the painted wall of the odd amusement, but there was no way to judge the thickness. How many layers? There were massive cracks running along the face of the dunes, some of which had been filled with gobs of thick paint, sealed up like scabbed flesh wounds.

From the street it was difficult to see that there were cavernous openings with painted arches on which the messages were written in various scripts, some of which were difficult to decipher. Mica didn't spend too much time trying to read cryptic renderings, quite aware that Erin was waiting for him. He looked back, but couldn't see her inside the car due to glare from the sun on the windshield. She was scowling at him, no doubt. Maybe even giving him the bird. Mica felt a sudden guilt for not listening to her. After everything they had been through, he should have stuck by her side no matter how interesting he found this place.

Turning, he peered through the painted archway to a whole new world of caves cut into the dunes. How could he not explore this?

Five minutes. That's it.

Through the archway, Mica found himself in a part of this bizarre roadside sculpture that could not be seen from the road. Opening out from above were a series of caves and tunnels carved and coated wholly in paint. Nothing so deep he couldn't see the end, but deep enough to rattle his nerves. The carved cubbies were littered with miscellaneous debris, almost as if each little room was themed, though Mica couldn't ascertain precise themes, and he was reluctant to find out. Suddenly he was feeling that maybe Erin was right. Maybe this place was better left alone. He remembered the documentary that featured Salvation Mountain. It was bustling with tourists, travelers, and passers-by. Climbing on the dunes, laughing, pointing in awe. Where were all the people? Even with a stark change in theme, there should be someone. This was the perfect meeting point for strung-out rocker kids or depressed Goths, wayward hipsters, or wannabe Satanists with a bend toward dominatrix. Why was no one there at all?

When the smell hit Mica, he knew he had to get out of there.

Nothing good came from an odor that was like natural gas mixed with death. This was a place animals came to die. Probably vandalized and painted to keep people away. He was foolish to roam around a place that was caked in runes of evil. He shouldn't need warning signs to see that he was in danger here.

The smell intensified. It seemed to be coming from all around. Mica decided to retreat, just get the hell out of there, but first he wanted to see what was in one of the little rooms carved in the dune. They reminded him of something seen in a natural history museum, a large diorama that displayed the way cave people lived hundreds of thousands of years ago. The closer he got to a particularly interesting little alcove in the painted dune, the more intense the odor became.

It was death, plain and simple.

Mica coughed. Words painted above the cave caught his attention: ALL HAIL GRAMMY VAL. He looked in at the mess, but wouldn't move any closer, for the smell was too horrid. He couldn't make out what he was looking at. It was like a mass of indistinguishable substance, glistening and moving. His eyes began to go out of focus, nausea sweeping over him from head to toe. The movement on the vile mass was random and chaotic. Focus returned in an instant, and that's when Mica realized that the movement on the mass were flies and maggots. Suddenly the death rank seemed that much worse, and though he still didn't know exactly what he was looking at, Mica turned and puked until he dry heaved.

"Mica, what the hell are you doing?" It was Erin's voice.

Looking up, Mica saw Erin standing beneath the painted archway that led to this bizarre and tragic series of tunnels and alcoves. He was salivating and spitting the taste of vomit onto the sand. Words would not come to him. He didn't want Erin to see this.

Erin scrunched her face, and then put a hand to her nose. "Jesus, what's that smell?" Then her eyes widened. Was that fear?

Mica wiped his mouth as he pivoted his head to follow his wife's gaze, unsure he wanted to see what had so suddenly filler her with terror. He'd fucked up. He knew it. They should have gone. There were warnings all around. They should have high-tailed it back to the hotel, back to Danni. Oh god, back to Danni.

What if they didn't make it back to Danni?

Behind Mica was a brutish woman with eyes like a devil.

Chapter Fourteen

anni sat in bed with a cushion of pillows between her back and the wall so she could sit up and watch TV. She was watching a silly teen comedy sitcom about kids who somehow managed to operate their own bakery. She'd seen all of the episodes before, but there wasn't much to choose from on the hotel cable. It was like they had every other channel that a normal cable service included. It was nice being left alone. It gave her the sense that they really trusted her, which was nice. On the other hand, she wanted her parents back soon. There was something unsettling about being inside a big hotel with all these other people. She was safe, the door was locked, but it was super weird to think that there were people above, below, and on the other side of the walls.

The television show went to a commercial break after some goofy cliffhanger that was funnier the first time Danni had seen it (there was this feeling as she watched the show that she was maybe too old for such childish programming and would prefer one of the prime-time adult comedies). The sound of a slide whistle caught her attention away from thinking about just how many people were sharing space with her in the hotel.

A swirling spiral appeared on TV, the kind of thing that could induce a seizure, with a clown face real small at the center that got bigger and bigger until it took up the majority of the screen. The clown, kind of a Bozo knockoff that would have looked great on a package of ice cream cones, winked. "He-hey, Kiddos! Come on out to the Salton Sea for the Greatest Show in the Desert! That's right! The super-duper awesome spectacular Circus Sideshow at the Circus Oasis!"

Calliope music danced in the background as the clown laughed and his head spun in wild circles bouncing around the TV set in a display of cheap effects. Danni, smiling in awe, couldn't put her finger on it, but something about the ad wasn't quite right. The colors were muted and lo-fi like old photographs she had seen of her parents when they were kids. Or better yet, photos of her grandparents.

A voiceover that was different from the clown (not nearly as enthusiastic and clearly reading the lines) said things like, "See elephants. See tigers. See dancing poodles. See the Strong Man bend steel!" With each attraction mentioned, a teaser image flashed on the TV. Danni could tell without a doubt that this was some kind of vintage commercial. "Aaaaaaand Valerie the Great!" At this, the image of a woman dressed in a ring mistress outfit with a whip, shiny black knee-high boots, red coat with tails. "Watch her tame a lion before your very eyes."

The ads that followed before the silly show came back for a goofy finale were more vibrant and brighter than the Circus Oasis ad. Something about that ad didn't fit. On top of that, those were real animals, and Danni knew that there were no longer real animals used in circuses. It was a vintage commercial, plain and simple, but why? Seemed kind of strange.

The stupid show she had been watching was forgotten about as her mind wandered. Danni was excited for the Big Top Show, but she would have liked to see a real circus like back in the day.

She understood why the rules had changed, and she wanted the best for the animals, but it sure must have been something to see. It was as close as she would ever get to these animals outside of the San Diego Zoo, which she had been to many times over the years. Danni loved the zoo, but she had her sights on a real-to-life African safari. Even at her age she understood that a trip to Africa was beyond the means of her family, but she could always dream. She had seen on TV once that there were parks where you drive through and the animals come right up to your car. That sure would be exciting. Just so long as the animals don't get replaced by robots. That would be Danni's luck.

The TV show was completely forgotten as Danni's thoughts drifted to her parents. They had been arguing a lot before they left for Circus Oasis. Seemed like a daily occurrence to hear them bickering and yipping at one another. Danni did her best to ignore the fights as if they would just go away. She knew money had something to do with it, but didn't completely understand how it was people who loved each other could bicker so much. Even on this trip there was a tension that Danni could feel radiating from her parents at times. It was difficult to ignore when she was in the same room. At home, she could go to her bedroom, put on head-phones and fade away into her favorite pop music. By the time she was finished listening to a few upbeat songs they would have cooled off and Danni could at least pretend that everything was all right, though deep down she knew better.

Divorce was a word brought up from time to time, one that Danni abhorred. She had a few friends whose parents had divorced, and though she had asked those friends what it meant, the answers did nothing to temper her confusion. Marci said that she got twice as many gifts for her birthday and Christmas. She spent the weekends with her dad. The glee displayed in her voice when she spoke of the extra presents had diminished when she talked about being carted around and doing "drop-offs" at fast food joints or the local Wal-Mart.

Danni feared her parents splitting up. When they started fighting in the car she thought that maybe it had something to do with the trip. Like it was her fault. She would have gone without the trip if that would help keep them together. She would do whatever she could to keep them together.

The mechanical sound of the lock on the door issued with a click. The handle turned, and Danni beamed at her parents' return.

The door opened, and her face dropped.

Chapter Fifteen

Bette walked along the edge of the Salton Sea, making no attempt to avoid fish bones. She couldn't have avoided them if tried. They were the sand. She wondered if there would be an attempt to remove the bone sand and replace it with clean beach sand. Perhaps if the Salton Sea became the Palm Springs of the Colorado Desert. Rich people needed somewhere to go, somewhere to spend money, spend a week away from the beach. The beach on the ocean, that is.

Bette tried not to envy the rich, and really she wanted for nothing more than peace. Envy played no place in that, but she was aware of how wasteful certain lifestyles were. Where would they dispose of the fish bone sand, after all? And where would the new sand be harvested? Those kinds of trifles meant nothing to most filthy rich people, and that bothered Bette more than the fact that she struggled in life, making it out to a desert to observe the wildlife and take samples, but making no money. It was never about money. Never had been. Never would be. She had always viewed life in simple terms. Decisions could be made by observing the good and the bad. She figured it was always just to approach life for the good. If her actions were guided by an appetite to better humanity, how could she go wrong?

It was while walking along beaches and in forests and around lakes that Bette did her deeper thinking. It was peaceful, even in the sweltering heat. And it was so much easier to think while alone with nature. And think she did.

The results of her biopsy hadn't come in yet. In fact, Bette had only gone to get the biopsy three days ago. That's why she didn't tell Dennis about the diagnosis. Her doctor said they found the cancer early. Said it looked like they could scoop it out and she would be in remission in no time. Said the biopsy and further blood work would confirm his suspicions. Said he'd seen this many, many times before. Early prevention is the best medicine. It doesn't appear to have spread yet.

Yet.

Was it spreading now?

Bette could go home. She'd collected enough specimens, observed enough wildlife patterns, and made pages upon pages of notes. She would do a proper write-up over a pot of coffee after telling Dennis about the Circus Oasis. About the strange things that had happened to her. About . . .

About the cancer. Tell him there was nothing to worry about, really, nothing. The doctor said so. Well, not much, at least. Just so long as the blood work and biopsy come back benign or negative or whatever. Just so long as it doesn't *spread*.

Standing there in the sun but not feeling the bathing heat, Bette stared out over the placid waters. Only five years ago it was thought that the Salton Sea couldn't come back from the state it had devolved into. The death and decay, the levels of salt so high no animal could survive. The disease, the pestilence. If the powers that be could take the cancer out of the Salton Sea, years of cancer, years of neglect, then surely her doctor . . .

Bette banished the thoughts of cancer and doctors, realizing that there was nothing she could to about it anyway. Not right now. She would check out the Big Top Show tomorrow night and head home in the morning. Before telling him about her trip she would share the diagnosis with Dennis. He deserved to know, and though it might not have been right to hide it from him for these few days, Bette felt that she had made the right move. There was no need for Dennis to worry about her, and she saw no reason to cancel the trip.

Under her feet, the smooth fish bone sand became more rigid. At first, Bette thought she was walking on small stones, but looked down and realized that the sand was becoming more substantial, more pronounced, speckled with little bones of gulls and tilapia. It was easy to forget about just how many animals died in this stinking desert sea once the bones had baked in the sun long enough to turn to sand. Seeing them like this made Bette sad. It reminded her of previous trips to the Salton Sea before the desalination plants. She used to bag and tag ice chests full of tilapia and various birds. For a while there, she was trekking out once a year. At the time, she never thought she would see this place on the mend. Seemed impossible. Just a nasty wasteland.

She glanced up, realizing now that she had walked all the way to Bombay Beach. Though there had been an effort to create nice, neat burms between the little pissant mobile home park and the water, it was still a place that reeked of Salton Sea's previous disgrace. She wondered if there would be an effort to demolish the park and build condos or something. Gotta keep up graces with what would likely become a flourishing getaway for the rich and famous. And maybe a little person who saved enough money for one of the shitty little motels that would be built on the outskirts. Because spending a chunk of your savings on a weekend out in the desert is a wise idea. It had to be. The rich and famous were doing it.

Bette stopped, closed her eyes, and inhaled warm air through her nose. A bit salty with a hint of dead fish, just a hint, mind you, but fresher than she'd ever smelled here. Was taxpayer money wasted on the desalination plant? Could it have been better used to eradicate hunger and homelessness? Inner-city violence and public schooling? Was it worth it, just for some new attraction out in the desert? Bette couldn't say, but as a woman who was concerned with wildlife of all sorts (humans included), she couldn't be more pleased at the state of the water and the shores surrounding it. The billions had certainly saved animal life, and Bette assumed they were thankful, in their own animal ways. Some of them wouldn't be so thankful gutted and scaled for dinner, but as much of an animal lover as she was, Bette could turn a blind eye on a bit of fishing. Just so long as the catch was eaten. And it took her a while to accept that. She'd fallen in love with Dennis before she realized how much he enjoyed fly-fishing. On top of that, Bette was no vegetarian. She condoned eating red meat and limited her fish and poultry intake. It didn't take much for Dennis to win the argument overfishing, and how could she deny him something that gave him such pleasure.

The rumbling of something beneath her feet brought Bette out of the daze she'd slipped into (seemed to be happening a lot as of late—since the diagnosis). She took several steps back, away from the water's edge. She thought she'd stepped on a snake for a moment, or one had somehow wriggled beneath her foot. That wasn't the case. Beneath her feet the sun-bleached fish and bird bones trembled, and for a second there Bette thought a train must have been coming. But there was no train that ran along the Salton Sea.

She stood there with a strange urge of panic rising from her toes up her legs, gooseflesh awakened in a ripple that gave her the most extraordinary chills. The chills mimicked the rattling fish bones, and their insistent rattle gave off the impression that thousands of large bugs were swarming beneath, causing the inanimate bones to dance. Bette wasn't one to scare at the sight of bugs, but the thought of so many bugs causing such a sudden disturbance was startling.

Extending one foot, Bette kicked some of the bones to see if there was something beneath. There was nothing but more bones, and they were rattling too. Dancing, squirming, clanking together. Dried fish tails, thin spines, delicate ribs, and then the larger bird bones. The sound was soft and yet unsettling, and then the dust of bones long ground into sand began to rise from the tumultuous movement. Bette instinctively stepped back the way she had come, watching the trembling ground. She covered her mouth and nose not so much from the smell (it was merely a salty, fishy smell like opening a bag of dried prawns from the international market), but as if she didn't want to inhale the dust. There was also the irrational feeling that she couldn't turn her back on the spectacle.

But she did. She turned and briskly walked along the shore until there were no bones beneath her feet, until her sandals made dimples in the sand. The bone sand. But this sand wasn't moving, and when she looked back she saw that neither was the area of shore she'd just come from.

In fact, there weren't even piles of fish and bird bones.

Bette closed her eyes, took a deep breath, and let out an exasperated sigh.

"You're losing it, woman."

Hearing her own words aloud was anything but comforting. Seemed kind of creepy and mad.

You shouldn't have come out here. Should have stayed with Dennis and told him about the diagnosis. It's eating you alive. Making you see weird stuff that's not even there.

Maybe the cancer spread to my brain. Maybe that's why I'm seeing this crazy shit.

Bette shook her head. Maybe she should just go home

tomorrow morning, be home by noon and fill Dennis in on everything.

One more look at the scene of the dancing bones. Nothing there but white sand.

Yeah, maybe it spread to my brain.

Chapter Sixteen

A t the whizzing sound of the locking mechanism, Danni smiled, pleased that her parents were home. It seemed a little early, but she figured that maybe they felt bad about leaving her alone. It was good to have the time to herself, but she was definitely more comfortable in her parents' presence.

The door opened. In rushed a man and a woman, but not Danni's parents.

Danni clutched the bed sheets tight. Her body ran with trembling fear. "Who are you? What are you doing in here?"

In the back of her mind there was some kind of irrational fear that someone would just come on into the room, but she didn't really believe that would happen. This was a safe place. With a lock.

"Don't worry," the woman said. "Your parents sent us."

Danni knew this wasn't right. There's no way her parents would have sent strangers into the room. Not unless . . .

As the woman approached, Danni clutched the bed sheets tighter as if they would do something to protect her. Her body tightened up the way one does when someone sees a car accident about to happen. She said, "Did something happen to my parents?"

The woman stopped as if some light went on in her head. She half glanced to the man standing behind her. Danni noticed the door closed behind him, and she didn't like that. A closed door meant she was completely closed off with these strange people. If she screamed (if there was some reason to scream!), a passerby in the hallway probably wouldn't hear her.

The woman nodded. "Yeah, that's it, your parents were in a car wreck."

The woman stood over Danni at the edge of the bed, and then it became clear to Danni who this woman was, or at least where she had seen her before. It was her hair. The colors. This was the woman Danni had seen out the window last night when she was sick. Danni's eyes averted the woman and landed on the man behind her. Danni immediately recognized him from the front desk. In some small way recognizing them made her feel at ease, but only for a second, only because recognizing them as hotel staff made it plausible that they had some kind of right to be there, but that feeling was momentary. Hotel staff paying her a visit made the idea that her parents had been in a car wreck that much more real.

The woman was on the other side of the bed now, the side Danny had retreated to. One hand was in a pocket, the other reaching out and grabbing Danni's shoulder in a gentle, comforting way. "I'm so sorry, honey, but they were in a very, very bad car wreck."

Tears welled in Danni's eyes. She didn't like the way this woman's voice sounded, almost like there was a spot of glee in there somewhere, as if she was holding back some sickening grin like she was about to burst into laughter. Danni shifted her gaze to the man once again. He stood sentinel at the door. No emotion. Just stood there. Scary. She looked back at the woman just in time to see the syringe slam into her leg. She yelped at the bite, but it was too late. The poison, medicine, drug (whatever!) was injected right through the bed sheets into her thigh meat.

The woman pulled the little needle out and put a finger to her lips. "Shhhhh. It's just to sedate you. That's all."

Face scrunching up, tears spilling not from pain, but from deception, fear of what was to happen next, what these people wanted with her, what had happened to her parents. Nausea came in waves and was replaced by a feeling like living in those haze waves that radiate from asphalt in extreme heat. Danni's mind became overwhelmed by a heavy, steamy sense of just fading away into nothing, like falling into a dream and realizing it. She fought the feeling, but the woman's face wavered, and there was nothing Danni could do to stop her mind from becoming encapsulated in sleep. Just before Danni slipped into unconsciousness, she asked, "Is the lion real?"

To this, the woman with the color-streaked hair wrinkled her brow. She said something like "what?" but Danni's eyes were closed, and she was out.

The woman stood beneath an archway, a menacing shape with sunlight gleaming behind her in colorful rays. Erin could faintly see her face, the open-mouthed smile, the evil slanted eyes of sadism. It didn't take a lot of deduction to tell that this woman was bad. No, beyond bad—she was horrible. She seethed something so awful Erin's stomach clenched just seeing her there. It was like stumbling upon a rattlesnake den covered in a black widow's web.

Mica stepped forward rather forcefully, as if he too sensed the extreme danger this domineering woman exuded. "Excuse me, but what the—?"

The sawed-in-half baseball bat came down on Mica's head so quick and forcefully that it took Erin a couple seconds to realize what had just happened. Mica fell limp on the ground and could have been dead he was so knocked out. Erin screamed and turned to run. She didn't know where to run, she just knew that she had to run before that little sawed-off bat crashed into her own head. She didn't even have time to see if Mica was breathing. It wouldn't matter whether he was breathing if she was knocked unconscious or killed. Someone had to get away. Someone had to get to Danni, to the police.

But there was no way for Erin and Mica to have been aware of the ambush. When she turned and fled, she smacked right into a man standing behind her. On impact with his barrel of a chest, a yelp was pushed out of her throat. He grabbed her, and she flailed. A look into the face of this man who held her arms with a grip like his fingers were made of steel showed her a face very different from the woman's. His eyes were almost piteous, almost warning, as if saying, hey, if you get out of my grasp you better get away, 'cause I'm not the one you need to fear.

"Get her!" the woman said. "Knock her out!"

It was clear who was in charge here.

It was the eye contact that stopped the man from hurting Erin. His eyes were almost kind. Almost. It was the bags of tired flesh around them, the wrinkles that seemed premature in a face that looked older than it should have, the nose that was enlarged and bumpy with skin cancer that made this man's appearance menacing. And, of course, the grip he had on Erin's arms, so tight she couldn't move.

Erin kicked the man's shins, and then one kick got him right between the legs. Her shin connected with the family jewels hard, and he sucked in a breath, his somewhat gentle eyes going wide and filling immediately with tears. He let go and sort of pushed Erin away. She stumbled, but managed not to fall.

"Goddamn it, Francis, you fuck!" the woman said. "Can't do a goddamned thing without fucking it up, can you?"

"She kicked me in the balls!" The words came out as if his throat was scrunched tight. Hunched over, he massaged his testicles through the fabric of his jeans.

"I don't give a shit if she ripped your goddamned balls off—hell, I did that a long time ago. Don't be a fucking pussy! You can't do a goddamned thing right, can you? Useless—"

Erin took this little argument as an opportunity to get away, but Grammy Val was quick on the uptake and lurched after her mid-sentence. She could bitch out her husband like a pro, but she was always very aware of her surroundings. Nothing got by Grammy Val. She swung the bat, but Erin was just out of reach. "You're not getting away, you goddamned bitch!"

Grammy Val was a hefty woman, but she was tall, and her leg span was impressive. This helped her run after snooping little shits who thought they could get away. She took mega leaps as Erin ran through what suddenly seemed like labyrinthine tunnels and caves painted all colors of the rainbow. Crudely painted images of skulls and crossbones, circus animals, and creepy clowns passed by. Erin just wanted some kind of escape into the desert, but seemed unable to find her way out. Grammy Val snarled at her heels and Erin screeched, and then she miscalculated and ran straight into a cave with no opening.

It was over. Erin knew that she'd messed up really bad. She stopped herself from running right into the wall of the cave (an eerie image of some screaming face with a yawning maw filled with a multi-colored spiral), but tripped over debris on the ground. The wind was taken right out of her lungs on impact. Using her hands to break the fall, Erin skinned the pad of her left palm pretty good. She went into a haphazard roll in attempt to avoid further damage. Her body smacked against the wall of the little cave (not much more than a large alcove, really), and there was a moment of still before Grammy Val's shrill voice slashed into her ears. In that moment, she was aware of the smell. It was all around and worse than anything she had ever experienced. What flashed in Erin's mind was the time they had rats in the garage and Mica caught three of them in one night on the half a dozen traps he set up. He'd tossed the dead rats in the garbage can, right along with the traps that had captured them. A few days later, Erin opened the can to toss in the kitchen trash and had a sudden urge to sneeze, which caused her to take a deep inhale just as she opened the garbage can lid. The smell was so horrid that she dropped the kitchen garbage and sneezed vomit out of her nose and mouth. This smell here in the glorified alcove was worse. By far.

As the unmistakable rank of death filled Erin's nostrils and her stomach roiled with the unstoppable urge to vomit, Grammy Val said, "Got yourself in a bit of a pickle, didn't you?" She capped that little statement off with a laugh so sinister it could have come out of the gaping maw painted on the wall. The evil woman stood at the mouth of the creepy little cave, sun haloing her body in a way that would make any other person appear angelic. But not this woman. She almost looked fiery.

The urge to vomit was real, and it was going to happen. Erin looked around as if she could find some kind of escape plan, yet she knew there was no hope. What she saw was enough to allow her gorge free, for she was sitting in a pile of dead animals. Rotted snakes in dizzying coils, the carcass of a coyote (or was that a dog), birds, wet bones. There was no holding back. Erin puked and Grammy Val laughed.

"You've got yourself a weak stomach, Missy," Grammy Val said. She took a step into the little cave, her eyes never leaving the sad, crumpled form of Erin amidst a stew of death, providing her own inner broth until there was nothing left to purge and all that came out were coughing dry heaves.

Grammy Val stepped forward. "I've got the stomach of a butcher."

Footsteps approach from outside of the diminutive cave. "Did she get away?" It was Francis. His voice was old and weak with a quality of shame, almost hopeful that the woman had indeed managed to escape into the desert.

Grammy Val pivoted her head and gave her husband side-eye. It was a glare that he knew well, one that seemed practiced in its fevered intensity. "Hell no. These are the ones Eve told us about."

Chapter Seventeen

When Danni woke, she was disoriented, thinking that she was asleep in bed at home, and then, realizing that she was in the Circus Oasis Hotel, she smiled, closed her eyes, and snuggled into the heavy covers. There was something comforting about being locked into the warmth of heavy covers with the air conditioning blasting in the room, only felt on her chill face. It was a feeling that was synonymous with staying in a hotel, not that Danni was all that familiar with the hotel experience. Outside of staying at a motel one year when they went to Disneyland—that place couldn't hold a candle to this one—Danni had never been in a hotel before. For her, just staying in the room was a pleasure, particularly considering how hot it was outside. The water might be fun, at least she could cool off, but going out in the desert like her parents had . . .

Danni's eyes opened with urgent realization. It felt as if the floor dropped from beneath and she was going to fall through all the levels of the hotel until she came crashing down onto the gorgeously tiled lobby floor, and even then she might drop further. It was a terrifying feeling that caused her heart to slam in her chest. She felt the throbbing of adrenalin and suddenly the covers felt like a horrible shroud locking her in place.

Tossing the covers aside, Danni leapt out of bed and slammed her back against the wall opposite the door, hitting the back of her head on the plaster but hardly wincing at the pain. That didn't matter. Nothing mattered.

Where's Mom and Dad?

Eyes darting across the room, to the little closet, the stationary table, the closed bathroom door. Where had those people gone? The man and the woman?

Images flashed through Danni's mind. The door opening, excitement that her mother and father were back, then seeing them. Two people. They shouldn't have been there. Danni had felt scared at the sight of them disturbing her peace, breeching the barrier of a locked door, for what use was a locked door when someone who shouldn't have the key, had a key. Her privacy had been disturbed, and they came in, closer, hovering over her. She'd smelled the man's breath: garlic and something funky like old cheese, or maybe aged cheese. The woman standing there. The woman from . . .

Danni, worried that the duo was hiding in the bathroom, moved toward the window and looked out over the big top tent like she had done the night before when she saw that woman below. Nothing outside. Just sun and desert and the large tent awaiting the Big Top Show.

Danni had been so looking forward to the show. That was the whole reason for coming out here. It was her birthday gift.

Where's Mom and Dad?

The room was empty, but the bathroom door was closed, and that scared Danni. If those people were in there, then what? What were their intentions? Just how long had Danni been out?

She felt her leg and shuddered when her fingers pressed the

tender flesh where the man jabbed her with the needle. He hadn't been gentle. It only took moments before she drifted off, but those moments were terrifying. The man's eyes were evil. The last thing she saw before she sunk into unconsciousness was the woman with the stands of color in her hair, snickering, and that was worst of all.

With light-footed steps, Danni crossed the hotel room as if there were floorboards beneath the tile that would creak. She was stealthy in her movements, like a child ninja. At the bathroom door, Danni paused and listened. There were no sounds from within and no light shining beneath the door. If they were in there then they were standing in complete darkness, and why would they do that? Would they really wait there in darkness until she woke, and then what?

Danni didn't want to open the bathroom door. She was afraid to. Because if they were in there, waiting in the darkness, then they were evil and had something nefarious in mind. They would attack her. Or worse. She was a smart little girl and her mother had told her that adults were not allowed to put their hands on her. Danni didn't completely understand how bad a violation could be at the hands of a sick individual, but she knew well enough that there were places no one were to touch. It was called molestation, and she knew that when someone did something like drugging a little girl, they might have that in mind. It was a lot like those stories about strange men in vans offering candy or toys, only this man offered a jab of something that put her to sleep.

Danni shuddered. The thought of what happened flashed sudden dizziness, and she had to palm the walls and lean in to avoid collapsing until the fuzzy feeling in her head left.

Canned laughter on the television brought a moment of clarity. Danni opened her eyes, and though she wished she would see her parents in the room and everything that happened was nothing but a horrible dream, there was no one. She was alone, and her bladder ached for release. She had to get into that bathroom. Besides, there was no one in there. No one would wait in the darkness like that. That would be crazy.

Eyes on the door handle as if expecting it to turn ever so slightly. The bad man and the evil woman within waiting for the perfect opportunity to strike.

Danni shook her head. No, they're not in there. That would make no sense. She was freaking herself out, over-thinking.

She grabbed the door handle and turned, hesitated with a keen ear for sound, and pushed the door open. A distinctly bathroom smell of soaps and lingering cleansers emanated, and the light from the hotel room illuminated the tiled floor, cherry wood vanity and granite countertop quite well. There was no one inside. As quickly as the relief washed over the little girl, the urge to pee became amplified as if someone had turned on a faucet. She rushed in, still had the foresight to close the door behind her, and did her business.

Leaving the bathroom wasn't nearly the challenge of opening the door in the first place. Now Danni was certain she was alone, but that didn't mean those people wouldn't come back for her.

Just outside the bathroom door, she saw the other door, the one that led out to the hallway. That door locked from the inside; she was sure of it. Doors could always be opened from the inside. That's how doors worked. They weren't designed to be locked on the outside. A glimmer of hope lit a spark within Danni's. She could leave the room and find someone to help her. Anyone. Maybe that nice woman she and her parents had run into a few times. What was her name? Beth? Barb? Danni would recognize her if she saw her. Even if she did see (Betty?) the woman, she could take the elevator into the lobby, and there would be people down there. She could go to the front desk and tell them to call the police.

Before she could make a mental chess game out of the situation and think three steps ahead, Danni grabbed the door handle and tried to turn it, but was unable to. She tried again, harder, almost furiously. And again, jiggling it this time, it was solid, pristine, locked.

Shaking her head, Danni took steps backwards until the backs of her legs met the bed. She stood there looking at the door in disbelief. Doors didn't lock from the outside. Not in houses and certainly not in hotels. What the heck was going on? *Where's Mom and Dad?*

The drone of mindless television programming changed into fluid, almost psychedelic calliope music overdubbed with a jolly clown voice advertising the Great Big Top Show. Danni watched the commercial in silence, almost fearing it for some reason. It didn't look right. The colors were muted like old photographs. It was out of place in comparison to every other ad. It was old. And those clowns were scary, even though they were laughing and excitedly talking about all the great things the Big Top Show had to offer.

The room felt empty. Where Danni had felt empowered and independent for being allowed to stay in the room alone, she now wanted nothing more than for her parents to be there with her. But they were gone, and something bad had happened. People had come in. They knocked her out, and what for? Why did they lock her in the hotel room?

And where were her parents?

In desperation, Danni looked out the window at the familiar sight of the big top. A feeling like she was as light as a dust mote crashed over her. It was as if she were floating out of her body, and yet there she was looking out the window. The strange feeling like her head was filled with helium persisted, and then a pair of lions walked out of the circus tent through the open flaps. Sun glinted off of their perfect manes of fluffy hair. It looked like someone had just ran a brush over these magnificent creatures. The sight of the lions brought Danni back into her skin, a stark shock into reality, for she knew they weren't supposed to be there, and it was quite clear that they were real animals. The animatronic versions couldn't look this majestic.

For a moment, Danni forgot about her predicament. She almost smiled, transfixed with the sight, however wrong it was to see such wild beauties unbound, and then a woman walked out of the circus tent. Bright colors peeked through thick blonde locks.

Danni's stomach dropped. It felt as if the woman would look up at her, directly into the very window, as if she could easily identify Danni's room from all the other identical windows in the hotel. Fear swelled like adrenalin, causing Danni to shake. The woman didn't look up. She didn't even regard the lions. She just walked right by them, almost right through them, and as she passed, they had sunk to the ground.

Mouth open, gaping, Danni watched the king of the jungle cower, shrivel, shake in the presence of a mere human being. She shook her head. *No, that can't be.* Just seeing the woman was frightening, knowing that she was a part of the sick little duo that had locked Danni inside. Was she so powerful that noble lions wilted in her presence?

Then something unbelievable happened right before Danni's eyes. The lions seemed to lose muscle definition. They shrank, thinned, turned into large, emaciated cats. The hair from their manes became matted and fell off in clumps. Their bodies quivered, and then they looked up, directly into Danni's eyes.

Breath caught in her throat, a shiver ran down Danni's spine causing gooseflesh to erupt across the backs of her legs. Tears filled her eyes, turning the world into a blur. Danni closed them tight, her jaw trembling, and then an overwhelming burst of emotion fueled by fear and solitude came over her like a tsunami. She bawled. Tears flowed freely, and through them she could see that the lions were gone.

Danni collapsed on the bed and whaled into a pillow, crying out, "I want my mommy, I want my daddy!" until the words were caught in her throat and choked there by deep, rattling sobs.

Chapter Eighteen

There was time for a drive before nightfall. The idea of staying cooped up in her room was loathsome for Bette. After her experience on the water, she was hesitant to rent another boat, and walking around in this heat was ill-advised. At least in the car she had air conditioning.

Tomorrow night was the inaugural Big Top Show, and Bette wasn't even sure that she would attend. Like that little girl she met yesterday, she had enjoyed circuses as a child, but with age and wisdom she learned to loath them as traveling torture camps of caged animals that were never meant to be in this country in the first place. She felt the same way about zoos. As a child, she had loved the San Diego Zoo. It was the greatest zoo in the country in both size and number of captive animals. Though the zoo had made advancements over the years in attempt to create larger enclosures to better mimic the animals' homeland, there was no excuse for humans to feel superior enough to stand around gawking at such beautiful creatures in captivity.

There were no cars on the road. Bette drove, more to calm her troubled mind and refresh, yet was also aware of any wildlife.

Something as simple as roadkill would have her stopped at the side of the road (as long as the sand wasn't too soft) for a quick investigation and a few notes.

Bette remembered the day she changed her view of life. She was sixteen, on a trip to the San Diego Zoo with friends. Her best friend Gracie had just gotten her driver's license, and that seemed like a great place to go that they couldn't have easily traveled to on the bus system from North County. At that age the zoo seemed like some kind of childhood novelty, but going anywhere in a car at sixteen was pure freedom. Bette and her girlfriends were walking through the zoo, laughing and eyeing boys when they came across the panther's cage. That's all it was. A cage. Smaller than the average living room. The poor thing was pacing back and forth, back and forth. Lonely. Isolated. Bette felt for the big cat. It should have been climbing trees and tearing through vast jungles. But no, it was just pacing, tossed a hunk of meat or a raw chicken from time to time.

That day Bette passed by the panther cage twice more, and each time the poor animal was pacing without end, yearning for release, yearning to run free. Bette thought about how that must feel. The closest she could come up with was being incarcerated. What crime did the panther commit?

After driving all the way to highway 8, which went west into San Diego and East into Arizona, Bette turned around and headed back towards the hotel. On her way back, she came upon a road that she'd seen before, one that seemed to go off into the desert. She had enough gas in the tank, so why not take a lonely road for a while? When she decided to return to the hotel, she could turn around on the two-lane highway with no problem.

This was a little-used road, evidenced by the soft desert sand that crept up on the sides in a wavy pattern like snakes flanking the left and right. This wasn't the kind of road you wanted to break down on. Merely pulling over to the side would prove disastrous for a vehicle without four-wheel drive. This sand was so soft and unassuming that it would sink a car right down to the chassis.

The open road did wonders to take Bette's mind off of her cancer diagnosis and breaking the news to Dennis. She wasn't all that great at compartmentalizing, but she was learning.

About a mile or so up the road she came upon a curious hill that was covered in paint. Bette vaguely remembered something about a desert attraction where some Jesus freak painted religious messages on some dunes, but as she drove by, she realized that this was something entirely different. A quick look in the rearview mirror. No one for what seemed like miles. Bette slowed to crawl by the bizarre attraction, if that's what it could be called. The colors were dark and muted with lots of red and black. The messages were bizarre in nature, stretching from satanic symbols to crude clowns to skulls to weird sayings that didn't really seem to mean a goddamned thing. There were even depictions of slaughtered animals.

Disgusting!

Bette wrinkled her brow and read one of the messages aloud: "Come one, Come all, get the FUCK out!"

Then she read the large words atop the hill to herself: *Damnation Mountain.*

A chill shot through her body like static electricity.

There were a few cars in what appeared to be a parking lot, but she wasn't about to pull in. There was nothing about this place that she wanted anything to do with. In fact, Bette had a sudden urge to head back to the hotel, but she didn't even want to enter the parking lot to turn around. She'd rather do a five-point turn down the road a way, just to be away from that strange place.

After passing, she looked in her rearview mirror and saw several animals standing at the top of the hill. Coyotes, a dog . . . Bette squinted into the rearview mirror. *Is that a—*

She slammed the brakes, unconcerned there may be a car careening down this forgotten highway, and turned in her seat for a better look, but the animals were gone. The coyotes, the dog . . .

. . . and the tiger.

All gone.

Part Three

Saturday

Katherine Lazar clutched the third and final box to her chest like a schoolgirl does her books. When she was given the boxes several years ago, she thought they were nothing more than mere tramp art. Maybe vintage tramp art, but nothing special. Not to someone who didn't have a house or apartment or even an RV to display them in. The fellow who gifted them to her was considered a magical man, though Katherine had never believed in such things. She figured he was a good talker with a swift tongue. There were plenty of those in Slab City, full of lies and tall tales and stories so preposterous they just might be true.

The man had given her the boxes and told her that they would help bring peace. He had said that he could tell she was a disrupted woman, that she had a lot she was running from, a lot she was hiding.

He was right.

It was all on display here on the side of the road, painted across a series of hills. Damnation Mountain. Just walking by filled Katherine with dread and fear and hate and anger, a swirl of emotions that hit her mind like a strong drug. Bad memories that went back thirty years. In all that time, the things her family got away with. It was horrible to think about.

Katherine didn't even consider herself a Lazar any longer. Hadn't in years. She had a first name, and that was it. Her family had a name too. She called them the Murderers. The vile images painted over the bluffs and dunes of Damnation Mountain were reminders of their ways. The torture. The exploitation. The dead.

Katherine clutched the box tighter. She had no idea what was going to happen. But she couldn't deny the pull she felt, the same pull the first two boxes filled her with, as if they had been lying in wait, dormant until the time was right. Katherine didn't know the significance of the boxes, but the previous two had been swallowed by both the waters of the Salton Sea and into the desert sands. After both occasions, she was left exhausted by her travels to get to those destinations, and on both occasions, she had passed out and been brought back by the lapping tongue of a dog that was gone each time she came to. Rascal. It had to be Rascal. He was the only dog she had ever owned, the only dog she had ever loved. After Rascal, Katherine had begun her life in Slab City and on the streets, the railways, wherever. Rascal was the last thing she had in any sort of domestic sense of living, not that her life had never been very domestic. Not back when the original Big Top Hotel was in business, and certainly not when she was a little girl forced to travel the country in a third-rate carnival.

Katherine couldn't help but glance at the images on Damnation Mountain as she passed. The bizarre messages in blood-red paint, the decapitated heads of lions and elephants, the creepy clowns. Things that she once loved turned into vile depictions of the macabre.

Onward and forward she walked, skin afire, red and blistered. Lips dry and cracked. Eyes red and burning like she'd been looking straight into the sun. Wherever the box led her, she would walk.

Chapter Nineteen

She woke up with a deep and satisfying yawn that was broken by the sudden sound of the television turning on. The music was familiar and loud enough to break any peaceful sense Danni could have had before remembering her predicament. On top of the calliope music a silly clown's voice pitched the Big Top Show, and Danni hated it. She had no lingering interest in this or any other big top. All she wanted was her family back.

She knew her parents weren't there, knew it as a fact, and yet she made a cursory look around the room, some last lingering hope that this had all indeed been a bad dream. Nothing had changed. In the time it had taken to get to sleep last night, Danni had traced the furniture and decorations of the room over and over again, learning the edges of the picture frames, the texture of the chairs, the exact items that were strewn across the stationary table (a pen, a blue Xeroxed restaurant menu, and her father's pocket change.

Nothing in the room had changed a bit. The door was still locked. The contents of the bathroom were as Danni had left them last night.

Slumped on the bed, Danni cried. Last night so many tears were shed that she figured she would run out. She remembered her mother telling her not to cry over spilled milk. It was one of those things her mother said a lot when Danni was a toddler. Eventually she asked why her mother said that when there had never been any spilled milk. Thus, it was explained that she shouldn't sweat the small stuff. It was explained that in life there would be plenty of things to cry about. A broken toy shouldn't be one of them. Danni had cried a lot when her hamster died, but she got over it. After that, crying over a stupid toy or sticking a sticker on the wrong surface seemed ridiculous. Here in the hotel room, those thoughts came to her as she cried. Danni the little girl who judged her tears, weighing their value.

Last night she had told herself that if she woke up alone, she was going to find a way out. She couldn't just lie there and cry until those people came back. This was bad. This was really bad.

Over the years, Danni had been taught lessons like stranger danger, don't talk to strangers, and to never accept candy or toys from strangers. Her mother had even taught her that if someone were to grab her, she should yell bloody murder and kick and scream, and if it was a man (because it usually was in cases of abduction), she was to kick him between the legs, and hard. Danni had felt prepared for those sorts of situations, and she was happy to have never had anything like that happen to her.

No one had prepared her for something like this.

After a moment of panic (more than a moment!), Danni closed her eyes, took deep breaths, and she began to calm down. Deep breaths were good. Her father used to "take five" when he became angry. He used to get really angry about what her mom called "small things", like fixing stuff around the house. His anger was never violent, just scary and loud with lots of curse words. He learned to "take five", and when he did that (what Danni could best describe as stopping everything for a few minutes to calm down), he would take deep breaths, sometimes even saying to himself, "Deep breaths. Deep breaths."

The oxygen helped. Danni was upset, but calm.

She approached the window. Just outside the circus tent, the lion stood strong, its mane full and glorious like flames burning around his magnificent and noble feline face.

The lion was looking up at Danni. She just *knew* he was staring straight up at her.

Danni wiped her eyes and gritted her teeth.

It was good to have the king of jungle veldt on her side.

Chapter Twenty

Erin woke up with a scream in her throat that she somehow managed to hold in. Wide eyes rolled around their sockets, taking in her surroundings. A room. Warm, but not hot. Not clean either. Old furniture with rips and poor attempts to patch with plaid fabric like the elbows of a clown's jacket. The unmistakable odor of grime she remembered from her friend Chloe's house when she was a kid. It was a distinctly sweet odor with dirty feet undertones deeply saturated in the carpet fibers. When they were teenagers, Chloe would spray perfume in her room in an attempt to mask the unkempt smell of her house, but had about as much success as a smoker piling on loads of fragrance in feeble attempt at covering up cigarette smoke.

Her head ached. Had she been hit on the head?

Erin closed her eyes tight and tried to remember what happened. Her mind was foggy and fragmented into random images and memories from the day before? The night before? Something before this room.

She could almost smell Chloe's perfume, the thought of which was mildly comforting, though that friendship ended years ago.

She opened her eyes again, but there was no way to tell the

time of day or even what day it was. The one window in the room was covered in foil.

Where's Danni? Where's Mica?

Heartbeat swelling, panic rising, Erin shifted from her position on the soiled carpet. The movement caused odd odors to erupt from beneath her, like horrible things happened in this room and the carpet had never been cleaned, just absorbing the sickness and lying in wait until someone disturbed the fibers. A deeper, sickening odor banished thoughts of Chloe's house when they were kids.

As Erin searched the room for her daughter, those images that taunted her mind became clearer, fighting their way through the pounding headache that thrummed in her head like a bad hangover. She remembered the ugly paintings on the side of that ugly Damnation Mountain. Remembered allowing Danni to stay at the hotel by herself, an offering of independence for a little girl who could be trusted.

Oh my god my baby's alone!

That terrifying thought was interrupted by something moving in the room. For a split instant, Erin's heartbeat raced at the sight of what appeared to be an emaciated tiger, and then, just as quickly, she realized it was a costume.

It was Mica dressed in a tiger outfit.

The sight was so absurd and incongruous that even the fear for her poor isolated daughter was momentarily banished.

What the fuck?

Mica shifted, but did not yet wake. In addition to the footie pajamas, complete with a hood over his head adorned with little tiger ears, his face was crudely painted with black and orange stripes. Even his bound hands were sheathed in paw gloves, bound as they were with something Erin couldn't see. Handcuffs? Chicken wire? Her own hands were bound, but not tight enough to be painful. Erin liked to be thankful for small favors, but she was having a hard time being thankful for anything right about now.

Looking up as if the answers were painted on the ceiling, Erin stared at the bumpy popcorn pattern of the acoustic ceiling. Tears welled in her eyes. She didn't want that, didn't want to cry. Crying solved nothing, and her little girl was alone in the hotel room. Terrified, the poor girl *had* to be terrified. Did she leave the room and report her parents missing? What then? Were the police called?

Tears breached the wells her eye sockets created like little concave bowls in her upturned head. They spilled down the sides of her face, and Erin was suddenly aware of how odd she felt. The warmth on her face like her pores were blocked, similar to a heavy grease paint makeup job at Halloween.

She flexed her fingers. Her hands were gloved in some kind of patterned fabric. The binding was some kind of cordage she wasn't familiar with. Only now did she notice that there was a fabric on her arms not of her own wardrobe, patterned in cheetah print. Looking down to examine her clothing, Erin was shocked to find that she was dressed in cheetah leggings and some kind of cheetah sweatshirt. Her hands immediately went to her face, almost instinctively. The greasepaint was sticky and warm. Her fingers came away with smears of black and yellow.

Erin trembled. Mica shifted and groaned. Voices erupted from a nearby room like a conversation that had began elsewhere while people walked from one location to another. The trembling intensified. Erin slapped hands over her mouth to stifle sounds she feared she wouldn't be able to choke down.

Mica groaned and shifted again, louder this time. Erin's eyes screamed in the silence, wide as she could open them. She crawled across the floor to him like a tripod with her bound hands. Close enough to coo him awake, she whispered his voice, staring intently. She hoped that when he opened his eyes and saw the look in hers, he would be inclined to keep quiet. Not that it mattered. She figured it was better to keep the illusion that they were asleep. Might buy them some time to attempt escape.

The voices in the next room continued bantering, or rather arguing from the sound of it. Abrasive voices, but indistinguishable. The nature of the conversation was lost on Erin, but it was disconcerting just hearing them in there. Whoever they were, they were sick enough to kidnap people and change them into animal patterned clothes, complete with a birthday-party-clown level makeup job. And what for? Nothing good.

Mica opened his eyes just a slit at first, as if the light in the room were attacking his retinas with daggers of fire, and then they opened wide. He reared his head back and smacked it into a cushion made of some kind of miscellany.

Erin put her hands up to her mouth in a prayer-like gesture and shushed him softly. In a whisper: "Shhhh. Don't say a word. We have to think of a way out of here."

Backing up a bit, Erin allowed Mica time to observe their surroundings the way she had after waking. The voices in the next room continued, a steady flow of more highs than lows, the type of people who were loud no matter where they went, attracting the attention of those around and demanding scornful looks. The kind of folks who slammed doors and held people prisoner for who knew what reason.

Grammy Val sat in a throne of a chair that was centered against a wall in the living room where any rational family would have put a couch. The chair had once been lush with deep red velvet that had since turned black over time, sort of glossy like the arms of an old couch in the house of a grease monkey. The details on the woodwork of this previously magnificent chair were custom, once afforded by a woman who ran a very successful circus-themed hotel. Clowns, tigers, balloons, lions, elephants, and more were carved meticulously into the wood, though now certain details had broken off. A tusk here and paw there, time and carelessness having won the battle.

"You can't keep on doing this shit," Tracy said to Grammy Val.

Val scowled at her daughter-in-law. "I'll do whatever the hell I like."

Tracy stood there shaking. She was so upset after finding out two of their hotel customers had been kidnapped that she didn't know what to do. She'd paced back and forth so much across the floor before Grammy Val and her sad throne that she just about wore a path through the carpet.

Edgar stood in the adjoining kitchen nursing a beer and checking his watch impatiently. He hadn't said much since his wife confronted his mother. He knew better than to get in the middle unless it was absolutely necessary. Both of them were tougher than he'd ever be and twice as threatening when pitted against one another.

Tracy tilted her head and kind of rolled it as if trying to soothe the stress out of her neck. She closed her eyes tight and then opened them and sighed heavily. "This is really bad. Don't you understand? Second day and you're already pulling some crazy stunts. I can't believe it!"

Grammy Val snorted and regarded her daughter-in-law the way a predatory animal observes lunch. "They shouldn't have been messing around where their noses don't belong."

"But they have a child."

"I like veal." A grin surfaced. Grammy Val's teeth were crooked and tobacco stained.

Tracy cringed. "You're a sick woman."

Grammy Val lifted herself out of the worn throne. The grin that had surfaced took residence on her mug. What once was a proud smile in the big top under the bright lights had, over so many stressful, depraved years, turned into something maniacal, something terribly vile and frightening. Tracy could hold her own, having known Val for so many years since she and Edgar had been together, but that woman could set Satan on edge, not to mention she was nearly six feet tall. It was everything Tracy could do to hide the fear from the intimidation she was swathed in.

Val's eyes, deep and dark and glittering, bore into Tracy's. "You know my motto, right?"

After a pause, Tracy nodded slightly. Her fear was showing, which was the very last thing she wanted. She knew what Val was capable of.

Val continued. "I do what I want, where I want, when I want. And I take orders from no one."

Tracy broke out of the fear-trance. In all these years, it stunned her how tight Grammy Val's grip was on everyone in her life. "No one's making orders. But you don't cut this shit out and you're gonna take it all down. All of this. Me and Edgar worked goddamned hard to get the hotel up and running again. You could show a little gratitude, you know."

"Gratitude?" Grammy scowled. "Fuck your gratitude."

Tracy cradled her face in trembling hands and shook her head. She looked across the room to Edgar, poor Edgar who took his mother's shit just like his weakling father. Edgar had the brains. If his mother listened to him, they could have been doing better a long time ago. The rest of the family were ghouls. Vicious, murderous ghouls who got their kicks in horrible ways. But not Edgar. The Circus Oasis was Tracy and Edgar's ticket away from this disgusting family, but he was forever under his bitch mom's control.

Tracy decided to shift the subject. "How did you find out about them going out to the mountain?"

Grammy Val strode through the living room toward the kitchen as if she hadn't heard the question. She grabbed a bottle of bottom-shelf gin from the sticky counter and poured two fingers into a random highball glass. "I have my ways," she said before taking a sip.

"I don't know why Eve looks up to you so much. What the hell does she see in you?"

Val raised her eyelids. "Freedom. Power. Confidence." A grin parted her lips, eyes gleaming. "What's not to like?"

Edgar sipped his beer and checked his watch. "Got to head back to the hotel soon, babe." A glance up to his wife. It was a sad glance, that of a man whose balls had been removed and placed in a jar long ago. A man who acted very different when not in the presence of the woman of whom said jar belonged to.

"What about the girl," Tracy said to Grammy Val, ignoring her husband.

Val smirked. "What about her?"

"Can't just leave her in the room."

"Like I said earlier, I like veal."

Chapter Twenty-One

There was something satisfying about staying in a hotel on opening weekend. Bette had never had this pleasure before. She had stayed in a lot of hotels and motels over the years while on research assignments, protests, humanitarian ventures, and more. Some of them were certified roach motels, and others were nice enough to live in. It was a crapshoot back in the day, but with the number of reviews on the Internet these days it was pretty easy to vet a place of business. She has seen a lot less roaches over the past ten years and was better off for it.

The mattress was comfortable, but a bit too stiff for Bette's taste. A backache was developing. Fighting it off with ibuprofen and, for now, winning the battle. Stiff mattress or not, she lay there thinking about the past forty-eight hours. So many odd things had happened. Visions. Premonitions. Something Bette couldn't really understand. Not a religious woman, Bette considered herself spiritual. She believed in possibility, but felt that there was no real way to know or even understand things like death or what lies beyond the stars. In her travels, she had seen a lot of unusual things, but nothing quite as surreal and uncanny as what she had witnessed here at the Salton Sea this weekend, and she had been to the

Salton Sea many times before without so much as an uncanny occurrence.

There was time to kill before the Big Top Show, but Bette was in no mood for the sun. Not today. If it weren't for the show, she would already be on the road. At least that's what she told herself. Maybe she was delaying. She loved Dennis more than anything. And for that, she wasn't certain why she was so reluctant to tell him about the cancer. No one wanted to talk about things like death and sickness. Getting older was an unavoidable reality. She would be upset were *he* to hide such a thing from her. Treat others as you would yourself and all that.

Letting out a deep breath, Bette slumped in bed, head tilted. She stared into a corner of the room, but she wasn't studying the texture of the wall. She was studying the texture of her life.

After too much deep thought that was beginning to evolve into restlessness (*probably aught to find something on the TV*), a flaw on the wall caught Bette's attention, drawing her away from the introspective mouse hole that was getting the better of her. On the wall in the corner was a decent-sized ripple that was either the sign of bad craftsmanship or a poor job at covering up some vintage 70s wallpaper.

On closer inspection, the wrinkle was more severe than Bette had initially thought. It was very much like old wallpaper that had been painted over and peeled away from its original seam. With even closer inspection of that particular wall, Bette realized that it was indeed wallpaper that had been painted over, and not professionally. She could see the seams through the paint. The wall was a flat surface with the ghost of a texture somewhere beneath the hidden wallpaper.

She fingered the corner where the seam had popped. It wasn't stiff as if several layers of paint had been used over the years to conceal it. She could peel it back if she wanted to, but that would only be a good excuse for the hotel to charge her for damages. It was a strange instinct, perhaps something to take her mind off of everything, but Bette resisted it and returned to the edge of the bed, where she collected the television remote and began channel surfing.

She flipped through a seemingly random assortment of channels with picture quality that accounted for a system that was basic, if not jerry-rigged for all of the rooms. Some channels screamed as she passed them; others whispered. Finally, she stopped on something, anything to fill the space with background noise. She glanced at the wallpaper pop in the corner, but her eyes lingered.

Now it was ripped and curled as if someone had deliberately pulled at it, as if Bette's instinct to tug at the peeling wallpaper had manifested itself.

The drone of some infomercial that teased at vintage rock and roll performances collected on twenty-seven DVDs for only five easy payments of $19.99 was lost on Bette, floating somewhere in her subconscious. There was no way that small corner of peeling wallpaper could have peeled away from the wall like that.

A sudden panic assaulted Bette as she feared that she had been the one to peel back the curl of painted wallpaper and somehow not even realized it. Had she entered some kind of fugue state? A trance? No, no, no. She had been sitting there channel surfing. It had only been a few minutes. There was no way this could have happened, and yet there she was, standing before the painted curl. It was about a foot in length. The curl, if unfurled, was probably another foot, creating a decent rectangle. She fit her fingers beneath the curl and gently pulled it out like looking at a scroll. The backside had writing on it. Bette wrinkled her brow and squinted her eyes to read the words.

"—azar Family Zoo Sidesh—" Below that in larger font: "—vation Mounta—" between the words were black and white Xeroxed pictures of animals that were difficult to decipher due to the nature of using a sub-par photocopy machine that didn't pick up the highs and lows of whatever picture had been used for the images. It was very much like a flyer for a local punk rock show.

Tilting her head like a curious dog, Bette pulled her fingers from the wallpaper curl and stood back. Strange that the flier was visible to her, as if it had somehow been on the backside of the wallpaper. That made no sense. The back of the wallpaper should have had a crust of glue, not a flyer for some roadside zoo.

After more consideration, Bette decided that this unusual little development gave her something to do, something to keep her mind occupied until the Big Top Show tonight. She pulled out her laptop and began searching for information about the Lazar family, and boy did they have a sordid history.

Chapter Twenty-Two

Mica and Erin huddled together in a corner of the room, listened to the conversation transpiring on the other side of the wall. They were thin walls, probably a mobile home. Sound traveled well, especially the voices of people who spoke loudly.

"What are we going to do?" Erin asked in a whisper.

Mica shook his head. "I don't know." He lifted his cuffed hands and tried to pull them through the little steel hoops without luck. It was more of a gesture to signify his helplessness than anything else. They had tried time and again to pull their hands through the cuffs. It wasn't happening.

"What about that window," Mica said, gesturing his cuffed hands toward the rectangle of tin foil.

"How do we get through it with our hands cuffed? We'll make too much noise. Besides, it looks like it's screwed shut."

Voices rose in the next room: "You're sick! This is the biggest night of my life. Don't you fuck it up."

Another voice. A woman's voice: "You should have never gone and remodeled the hotel. You're wasting your time. We have all we need right here."

"Bullshit we do. We live like pigs, like roaches. You want to live like this? Really?"

"I'm done with the hotel. I've been done with it for years. I like what I do for a living."

"A living!" The man sounded genuinely exasperated. "You make no living. You're just scraping by, and you're doing horrible things. We thought that maybe we could change that. Make things more like they used to be."

The conversation became too muffled to make out.

"What are they going to do to us?" Erin asked.

Mica shook his head, opened his mouth as if to answer, and then closed it. Shook his head some more.

"They're going to kill us," Erin said. "I just know it. What's going to happen to Danni?"

The gloss over Mica's eyes became more than his eyelids could contain. Tears spilled down his face. All it took was thought of his daughter and he was jelly. Poor Danni, alone, or maybe in police custody. She could be anywhere. She could have wandered off after her parents didn't return. Wherever she was, the little girl was probably scared half to death.

Mica sniffled and used his bound hands to wipe tears off his cheeks. "We have to do everything we can to get out of this. We have to do it for Danni. She needs us. We need her."

Now Erin was crying.

The man's voice erupted from beyond the wall. "There's going to be reporters and critics here tonight from major Southern California papers and even some national websites. You gotta stop living in the past, dammit! The things you're doing are terrible. Fucked up. We're not going to keep covering for you, and I don't want you bringing Eve down this bad path. She can have a better life."

"She likes it," the woman said. Her words were soaked in poison.

Again, the conversation permutated and became indistinguishable.

Erin leaned her head into Mica's shoulder and sobbed. "What are we going to do?"

Mica's voice was heavy with emotion. "We're going to get to Danni."

Chapter Twenty-Three

As the hours moved on, Danni spent most of her time standing at the window looking out over the circus tent, lamenting the fact that she was going to miss the Big Top Show and crying over her parents. Situations and scenarios played through her mind, many of them dire, terrible scenes of loss. Other thoughts were more heroic and valiant. She breaks out of the hotel and finds her parents, and they all walk into the sunset, happily ever after. The end. Let's have ice cream.

But then she would see her mother's suitcase and reality set its hooks in. She would see the loose change on the stationary table and think of her father. Tears were shed by the bucket load, so many tears. How could one body produce that many tears? Then Danni would gather her strength, grit her teeth, and she was ready for battle. She was the lioness.

Outside, people milled about taking pictures of the circus tent with their phones, pointing at the enormous banners that had been hung advertising the various events, the animals, the excitement that Danni was going to miss. Everyone looked so happy, even in the sweltering heat. They ate ice cream cones bought from a clown that was vending out of a little pushcart. They smoked cigarettes and sipped cola. They squinted when they looked up, and no one seemed to notice the little girl in room 635, alone and yet surrounded by so many people.

She watched them come and go, all preparing to return later that evening for the show. There were a lot of people, more than she had seen last time she was out of the room. The place must have been packed, and yet here she was, locked in a room with no means for escape, no way to contact the outside world.

As Danni watched the mingling of the public, she was looking for two people in particular. It wasn't that she really thought she would see her parents out there having a jolly good time with the others, but that she had to have something to hold onto. Maybe, just maybe she would see them returning from wherever they had gone, dazed and sullen, happy to finally be back to the hotel where they could reunite with their daughter.

But they weren't down there. And they wouldn't be. Danni knew this just like she knew that wherever her parents were and whatever situation they had gotten into was bad, very bad. Deathly bad. Things like this didn't happen in real life, and when they did, the results were super negative.

Danni reminded herself to remain positive, but it was getting harder and harder to do so.

Outside, a sweaty clown smiled and moved around like his spine were made out of rubber. He seemed to be bothering more people than he was amusing them. Balloon animals for the kiddies (Danni certainly didn't consider herself a kiddie, but would have gladly accepted a princess crown or even a balloon sword were she out there), a flower on his over-sized lapel that shot out misty squirts of water, and absurdly large pockets with little trinkets and candies for the children.

Danni sighed and fought back a fresh onslaught of tears. *Stay strong,* she told herself.

As she watched the meandering crowd something spectacular

happened. It was something she had seen before, something shocking that she was strangely becoming used to. Padding through the crowd with lazy self-assuredness was the lion. It sat on its haunches at its usual place and looked up at Danni. No one seemed to notice the noble creature. Danni noticed that its movements were far too sleek for it to be some kind of animatronic. It was real. Or perhaps an illusion, a figment of her imagination. That didn't seem likely since Danni had seen it before, just as clear as day, but the people around the lion walked on by without so much as acknowledging the beautiful animal.

The lion stared up at her. She just knew it had to be looking at her. She wanted to cry, but had to stay strong. *Stay strong.*

Stay lion strong.

The lion opened its mouth as if yelling or yawning deeply. Danni gasped. It had no teeth. They had all been removed, leaving its maw a rigid landscape of soft gummy flesh.

Danni's heart beat faster and faster. The lion closed its mouth and stared up at her with sad eyes. Even the king of beasts was no match for the cruel and unusual torments of the king of all freaks: the human. Someone used their brains to crate an animal that could be led around and trained without a real means to protect itself. She couldn't see from her vantage, but Danni figured it had no claws either.

The image of the lion's gaping, empty maw flashed in Danni's mind, something traumatic that couldn't be unseen. And then she remembered the tooth she found beneath the nightstand. Her eyes went wide as she sucked in a breath.

Clamoring to the floor Danni crawled over to the nightstand and reached under it. At first, she felt nothing, and then she found something. It wasn't a tooth, but the smooth gray magnets she had lost the night they got there.

Magnets in hand, Danni returned to the window and looked

out, but her lion was gone. She closed her fingers around the magnets tightly.

I'm going to stay lion strong.

Chapter Twenty-Four

Though Bette's research on the Lazar family wasn't quite as lucrative as she would have liked, she *did* dig up some rather interesting tidbits going back all the way to the original incarnation of the Circus Oasis back in the seventies.

Bette closed her laptop. She pushed her fingers into the sides of her head and rubbed her temples in a circular motion. A stress headache was burrowing in. She knew stress headaches well going back to her previous job in claims at an insurance agency. Her high-ups were obsessed with finding any and every way not to pay out a claim. The pressure to find even the slightest sliver of fraud was so intense that she would often go home with her head feeling like a cracked egg. Eventually she was laid off (something that was constantly feared under the employ of smaller insurance firms), and that's when she decided to devote the rest of her life to something she was passionate about. Her work with various animal rights groups was more charitable than not, and that was perfectly all right. On this trip they covered her hotel and gave her a stipend for food and materials. If her discoveries warranted further action, there was a legal team working with the organization that would file any necessary suits with the Circus Oasis and or the Salton Sea Authority Board of Directors.

It was six o clock in the evening. Time had become nonexistent while Bette researched. It was nice to have something to get her mind off of everything that had happened, but now that she was sitting in a silent hotel room her mind insisted on going back to the strange paw prints in the sand, the animal she could swear she saw in the lake, the tooth that little girl found under the nightstand. Of all the strange occurrences, that one came back to Bette most frequently. There was physical evidence. It couldn't be sloughed off as mere hallucination or a trick of the light. It was easy to brush off as a piece that had fallen off of decorative art, but Bette had been paying attention as she walked through the hotel, and she had yet to see any artwork that utilized animal teeth. Outside of shark teeth, she was fairly sure that using animal teeth in artwork was frowned upon.

To take her mind off of the strange happenings, Bette thought about what she had learned. What had she been looking for in the first place? Did she think she would have enough dirt to press some kind of charges against the hotel? And what for?

Outside of petty crime and one account of animal cruelty, there wasn't much of a criminal history for the Lazar family over the past thirty years. Bette found this out by paying for a background check after going through several articles on the Circus Oasis and the Salton Sea itself that, in one way or another, featured the Lazar family. They came from a long line of carnies that used to travel the country and eventually settled in the Salton Sea, where they never left. It was questionable how they survived over the past thirty years. There wasn't much information on the Salvation Mountain Roadside Zoo. Apparently, it had been an attraction back in the eighties, but there was little evidence and only a handful of grainy pictures.

It was the animal cruelty charge that piqued Bette's interest even more. She dug up an old San Diego Union Tribune article from '78 that centered on the closing of the Circus Oasis. The reasons for closure cited was lack of income incurred after heavy storms swept through the Salton Sea, causing severe damage to neighboring businesses that resulted in a massive drop in tourism. Fellow entrepreneurs counted their losses and moved out of town, leaving the battered remains of the Salton Sea's former glory. Destroyed boat docks, a motel with half the roof caved in, toppled palm trees, and the beginning of an annual event that was known as the fish die-offs. The rancid stench of hundreds of dead fish that lined the water's edge was the final nail in the coffin of the once lucrative and prosperous Salton Sea as any kind of getaway destination.

The Circus Oasis attempted to ride out the storm, so to speak, but in the end, it was one local bar and a small market that survived due to the proximity to Bombay Beach, the only community around the Salton Sea too poor (or perhaps just too stubborn) to leave. The writer of the article spent a paragraph on the last dregs of the Big Top Show, describing the turnout as "four lost souls, myself included, who must have stumbled in by mistake." Of the show itself he wrote: "A dismal attraction that gives third rate carnivals gold status, the performers were sad and uninspired, the animals emaciated and on the verge of collapse, the show as a whole enough to cause this reviewer to consider hari-kari."

Standing at her window, looking down on the people laughing and stuffing their gullets with popcorn and cotton candy as sweat poured down their faces and saturated their underarms, Bette checked her phone for the time.

The Big Top Show began in one hour.

Chapter Twenty-Five

Hours passed in isolation. Mica and Erin sat together on the floor, whispering and then stiffening up when voices became louder in the other room. There were many voices and thumps like barbarians stomping through the house. With each heavy thud, Mica and Erin cringed and stared at the door expecting the worst.

"I'm sorry," Mica said in a whisper.

"Sorry?" Erin's wisp of a voice cracked.

"For lying to you. About work. It wasn't right of me. I've been hardheaded. I should have listened to you."

Erin opened her mouth as if to respond, and then closed it. This wasn't the right time for a smart-ass quip. But then again, this wasn't really a good time for Mica to be apologizing for his misgivings.

Mica continued: "I can be so hardheaded about things sometimes. I sit here, and all I can think about is Danni. What she's doing, if she's all right, where she's at. Why wasn't I thinking about her future when I was lying to my family about working?" His voice wavered. "What's wrong with me?"

"Right now, I don't think it matters. Getting out of here

matters. We can fix everything else once we get out of here. I've hated you a lot lately, Mica. I've thought terrible things. Things I regret." Erin looked into Mica's eyes, hers shining in the dim light, his already spilled over with fresh tears to match the previous saturation thoughts of his daughter had caused. "I love you. If we can get through this, we can get through anything."

Mica did his best to form a smile, but he was too wrecked, so he nodded as more tears ran down his face, gliding over streaks of greasepaint. Lifting his cuffed hands, he put his arms around Erin, and they held one another tight.

That's when the door opened.

Mica frantically pulled his arms over Erin's head, mussing up her hair a bit, and they both huddled together. They hadn't intended on cowering. It was more of a reaction to being caught in a tender moment, unprepared for the inevitable. It was fear of what was to come next.

At the door, Grammy Val stood in full ring mistress regalia. Black pants tucked into knee-high black boots, a bright red tailcoat and top hat that was decorated with teeth and animal bones. She held a coiled whip in her right hand. Opening the finger of said hand, she allowed the whip to unfurl while keeping a grip on the handle. A simple maneuver practiced to perfection.

Erin sucked in a breath and began shivering, sticking close to Mica. All previous plans they had thought up, all the courage they bolstered had deflated in the face of this maniacal woman and her whip.

Grammy Val stepped into the room. From behind her, a young woman in a flashy sequined gown entered. Both Mica and Erin recognized her by the multi-colored hair as the desk clerk from the hotel. In her hands, she had two leather leashes. On her face was the most disturbingly gleeful smile, so polar opposite of the snide, sneering woman she had been while working the hotel's front desk.

The sound of the whip-cracking was so sudden and startling that Mica and Erin both yelped. The end of the whip made brutal contact with a plastic bag filled with miscellany, ripping the bag open and spilling the contents onto the floor.

Val said, "She's going to put those leashes on your collars and lead you into the main event. You make so much as a wrong move and I'll rip you open, do you understand?"

Mica and Erin nodded in unison. They were shaking, sniveling, terrified.

Eve stepped up to the duo and clicked the leashes onto leather collars that had been placed around their necks when they were unconscious and had been dressed in animal costumes. She did this without hesitation or fear of retaliation. Mica could have used his hands and swatted the woman across the face, probably knocked her out, but a carefully placed crack of that whip could lacerate his neck. It wasn't worth the risk.

"Are you ready for the show, my pets?" Grammy Val asked.

Neither Mica nor Erin responded, both uncertain what, if anything, they should say to this woman. Erin recognized her from Damnation Mountain. She was as vicious as an angry rattler and unpredictable to boot. Now, armed with a whip, there was no telling what she was capable of. People who abducted other people were assumed to be capable of anything. How else could this situation come out in the end other than death or prolonged captivity, which would probably be a far worse fate?

Grammy Val's eyes narrowed. "I said who's ready for the show?" She poised the whip like a nonverbal threat.

Erin swallowed hard. She opened her mouth to say something, but words wouldn't come.

Mica nodded. "Yeah, wah-we're ready for the show."

Mouth agape, Erin shot her husband a look of desperate horror, to which he returned the expression with one of his own: abject fear and terror. In those minute glances, the Burkheads knew that they were about to embark on something horrible, and that they would need every sense about them. Mica was right to speak up. It was better he said something before the whip spoke up.

Grammy Val slipped into a performance, completely changing her banter and attitude as if on command. "Right this way, my pets. The show is about to begin. The audience is waiting with bated breath."

She gestured toward the door. Again, Erin and Mica had a decision to make. Stand up and exit the room or remain cowering in the corner, maybe see if the whip was a smooth talker or a screaming banshee.

Mica's eyes darted toward his wife without actually moving his head, sort of like sneaking a glance. They were relying on one another, reading each other's intentions. It wasn't a "save yourself" situation. They were a unit. If they were going to get through this, they were going to get through this together.

Mica offered the slightest of nods, a gesture that said, *yeah, we better get up and head through the door. Our lives depend on it.* Erin did the same, a nod so soft and gentle it was for him alone.

Mica and Erin stood, now feeling the weight and awkwardness of their absurd costumes. If there hadn't been air conditioning they would have been drenched to the bone in sweat. As it was, with the greasepaint, they were incredibly uncomfortable and sweating from nervousness and fear. Everything they had imagined in the past several hours was gone. Now was real, and they had no idea how far things would go.

The next room was brightly lit with all variety of lamp and wall sconces. The warped atmosphere in the room was too much for Mica and Erin to take in. They were surrounded by people sitting in couches, folding chairs, and standing against the walls like young boys at a school dance who were too shy to ask a girl to the dance floor. They ate popcorn and sipped soda, crunched peanut husks and discarded the shells at their feet with no regard for the carpet. There were smiles and cheers as the sad cheetah and tiger made their way to the center of the room.

Grammy Val walked up behind Mica and Erin, taking her place proud and standing tall. Though the walls were stained, and the surfaces covered in dust and filth, her ring mistress outfit was impeccable, from the shiny top hat down to her polished boots. Eve followed, closing the door to Mica and Erin's previous hell behind her.

The audience was a sordid mix of people from all walks of life. Unkempt and inherently mean-looking, the people of Bombay Beach were nothing if not living on the edge of despair and personal destruction. These were people who would get off on all matter of bizarre ritual just to take their minds off of how pitiful their lives had become. These were people who drank too much, swore like bikers, and cheered when the bad guy won. This was a crowd that could turn on someone. This was a fight just waiting to explode after one wrong word, one too many beers, or a mere misunderstanding.

This was some scary shit.

Chapter Twenty-Six

When minutes ticked off like a collection of hours, time was redefined. Time stretched as Danni waiting in the room for something, anything to happen. Yes, preferably her parents coming back, but how long could she wait there? Her stomach twisted into knots of hunger that couldn't be satiated with the package of saltine crackers her father had saved after dinner last night and the half a candy bar that was on the stationary table. She had plenty of water from the tap, but there was only so much water she could take in.

Over the past several hours, Danni had scoured the entire room, hoping to find her tablet or maybe one of her parents' phones. She thought that perhaps one had fallen behind the bed or got caught up in the sheets. It was an act of futility, but the exhaustive search took up what would have otherwise been idle time looking out the window or thinking about the many disastrous outcomes of this hotel room captivation.

Hope was just about gone and fled the room, the building, the Salton Sea! If someone didn't come in here and murder her, she would slowly die from hunger, which sounded awful. Not that murder was a viable solution. Besides, her parents should have been there by now. There was no excuse. Something bad had happened, and Danni was beginning to think that her parents' disappearance had something to do with the people who had come into the room.

About an hour ago, Danni had stopped looking out the window. It was torture to see all those people laughing and yucking it up. They were happy. They were free. She wondered if there was anyone else being held captive inside one or more of the other rooms? Was it just her? Were her parents in another room? Danni couldn't look out over the crowd any longer. The window was sealed shut, which, her father told her, was a law in California, probably so people wouldn't fall out or do something stupid. He didn't explain what doing something stupid meant, but Danni had a good imagination. There was a story about a boy named Justin at her school who supposedly saw a ladder leaning against his house and climbed on the roof. He thought he could fly and jumped. Broke both legs and a few ribs. People did stupid stuff for sure.

Danni spent a lot of time staring at the door handle. She tried opening it several times without luck. How could hotel room doors be locked from the outside? Even a nine-year-old girl knew that was dangerous. What if there was a fire? An earthquake? How would she get out?

The thought crossed her mind, not for the first time, that perhaps she could trick the lock. The key card had impressed her so much that she'd asked her father how it worked. He said that the locks were magnetized.

Magnetized.

Danni had set the little gray magnets on the bed after what seemed like hours fidgeting with them in her hand. She found them in the same spot where she had found the lion's tooth (she was sure that it was a lion's tooth, and not just any lion, but *her* lion). *Lion strong.* Maybe the magnets could help her.

She stood up and approached the door, an inkling of hope rearing its head where hope had fled hours ago. She wanted to hope, to believe that there was a possibility for escape, and it didn't take much to get the butterfly feeling in her stomach. She didn't quite know what to do with the magnets, so she placed them on the door handle and began moving them around, listening closely for the sound of a lock, something to indicate that she was overriding the lock.

Nothing happened. The hope faded quicker than it had come back to her. Helplessness swarmed, and then something happened. At first, she thought it was the lock, and it was, but then the doorknob turned all by itself, and she knew in that split second that someone was coming in—*Mom and Dad!*

Danni stepped back. The door opened, and she could see that it was not her father. It was the man from last night. Without even thinking—

LION STRONG!

—Danni used all of her might and pushed the door, catching the guy by surprise. The door smacked him in the face, and hard. The sound of his head getting hit was loud, startling. The door was closed again. The sound of his body falling to the hallway floor resounded.

Danni's eyes went wide. She covered her open mouth with one hand, shocked at what she had just done. Even though she knew the man on the other side of the door was bad, she felt a pang of shame for pushing the door into his face like that. She'd never done anything like that before. Never had to.

Just remember that he locked you in here. What do you think he was going to do when he got in?

You're lion strong!

Her mother had told her about what bad men did to little girls, and she didn't sugarcoat it. It was a dialog that was easy to have whenever her mother would get an Amber Alert on her phone.

Danni didn't completely understand all the ramifications of a kidnapper, a potential rapist, but she knew it was bad. Really, really bad. That man behind the door was one of them.

After convincing herself that what she had done was okay, Danni became hyper-aware that she had very limited time before he woke up, and when he woke up he was going to be angry with her. Suddenly she felt stupid for doing what she had done, no matter how instinctual and necessary it seemed at the time. She was locked in the room, after all. Just waiting for him to wake up, and then what? He would be pissed off, maybe have a headache from getting a door pushed into his face, and he would have it out for her.

A few of her magnets had fallen off of the door handle when she smashed it into his face. They didn't work to breach the magnetized lock, but that didn't mean they weren't important, because Danni was sure her lion had helped her to find them for a reason. To get her over to the door. To be there when the man came back, so she had a fighting chance. And didn't he open the door? He would have had to unlock it.

Danni grabbed the door handle and twisted, sure it would be locked in place and doom her to wait in torture as the bad man on the other side woke from his stupor on the hallway floor. But no, it turned, and she opened it.

The man lay on the floor, his nose ruptured and bleeding onto the carpet. At the sight of what Danni had done, she sucked in a gasp of air, shocked. Her shock was short-lived, for she knew the intentions of this man. She knew he had something to do with her parents' disappearance. She had no pity for him. She was lion strong, and freedom was only steps away.

Closing the door, she stepped over his body and ran. She turned a corner and was faced with a bank of elevators. After hitting the DOWN button frantically, fear of the bad man coming around the corner caused shivers to roll through her body. What if she got into the elevator just as he turned the corner? What if he got in with her?

A bright green EXIT sign caught her attention. The stairs! Danni leapt across the hall from the elevator bank and opened the steel door that led to a warm concrete hallway of stairs. She headed down.

Chapter Twenty-Seven

So many people laughing and eating popcorn and hotdogs downed with crisp soda and fizzy beer. Clowns with bright red grease paint grins, waving at children and feigning exaggerated expressions of sadness and glee. Glitzy women walking around selling peanuts and cotton candy like old-fashioned cigarette girls, all bright smiles and slow sauntering through cheery crowds.

Unable to keep herself away from the spectacle, Bette was in the middle of it, inhaling the odors of mustardy hotdogs and cigarettes and even the occasional whiff of weed. The lights around the big top tent were bright enough to attack the shadows and illuminate the area like the hotel had its own patch of sun, which was eerie to observe from the outskirts of the commotion, for the rest of the outlying desert was dark, only illuminated by a clear sky of stars like millions of tiny holes poked into the black backdrop of the universe. In that moment, it seemed as if the glowing big top tent could be seen from outer space, like it would rival Vegas, which was preposterous.

Bette was nervous, and she didn't quite know why. It was as if all of the strange occurrences from the past few days had led up to this night. No one else seemed to bear so much as a concern. Though this should have eased Bette's mind, she was on edge. Standing away from the crowds, she took it all in, scanning faces and judging the level of good cheer. These were generally happy people, locked into their own vices and doing what people did at circuses. Kids laughed, parents warned about climbing this and slipping on that. More laughter.

So why did Bette feel so uneasy?

Where are those nice *people? Where are the Burkheads?*

It would be comforting to see someone she had met over the course of the past few days. At this point, she felt alienated from the crowd. What was she doing here? Did she really want to see the Big Top Show?

Leaning against the wall of the hotel, Bette looked up at the stars as if seeking guidance. She was overreacting, that's all. Should have gone home earlier. She would be with Dennis having dinner right now, away from this bizarre circus atmosphere. Away from the odd memories of things she could only attempt at understanding.

She saw a shooting star in the sky, brilliant on a desert backdrop, and then another. If there was going to be a meteor shower, she was going to step away from the big top tent for a better view. There was nothing like witnessing a meteor shower in the desert on a clear night. She would get more out of a natural phenomenon than a cash cow manmade circus.

Three more shooting stars, and something was off. They swarmed together rather than cascading through the sky as shooting stars were apt to do. Bette had never seen anything like this. The swarm of stars appeared to be way out in the galaxy, and then it was closer. It couldn't have been composed of stars. There was no way. As Bette watched the swarm move and shift, some of the so-called stars breaking away and swirling about like embers in the wind, she was acutely aware of what she was watching. The behaviors of what she thought were stars in the sky was, in fact, a flock of birds.

The flock came closer. The crowds were oblivious. No one seemed to notice the phenomenon. And they were indeed birds, glowing with a faint phosphorescence. They weren't supposed to be there. Worse yet, the closer they flew, it was quite clear the flock was composed of several bird species, which was something not seen in nature.

Bette looked away. Her anxiety rose. She scanned faces for the Burkheads. For some reason she thought she could talk to them about the strange things she was seeing, like maybe they could sympathize, like maybe they had seen weird things too. That little girl had found the animal tooth in their room after all.

Keeping her eyes away from the sky only did so much to ease her mind, for there were land-borne specters flitting about unnoticed by the other attendees. They seemed to emerge from the shadows far beyond the reach of so many bright lights surrounding the circus tent, rearing up and fading into the ethers. Large cats, lions, tigers, and the like. Smaller animals like dogs or coyotes. And then the magnificent giraffes and even an elephant.

My god I'm losing my mind.

These animals only showed themselves in fleeting glimpses, like flickering images from old one-reelers that flashed with an ethereal glow over a desert landscape from some giant projector. That was an attempt as rationalizing such phenomenon. The problem was that they were three-dimensional. Maybe there was some sort of holographic element to the show. Maybe that's what she was seeing.

But nobody else seemed to notice, and what Bette saw would most certainly have been noticed.

Still no sign of the Burkheads.

Chapter Twenty-Eight

Grammy Val cracked the whip with practiced precision. The popping sound it made startled Mica and Erin. Their fear and trembling resulted in cheers and catcalls from the lowlife audience. Toothless maws swilled beer. Greedy hands shoveled fists of popcorn, half of the stuff breaching mouths and falling to the ground. A sticky-faced child with eyes like Charles Manson drooled over a dense-looking stick of cotton candy that probably came from a dollar store.

Standing tall and proud, Grammy Val nodded as her diminutive crowd cheered her on. She took in each and every face. These were the people she lived with, the people who had supported her odd sideshows and roadside zoos. People who had been conditioned to enjoy depravity over the years of living like swine. People she had manipulated.

"Get ready for the greatest show in the Salton Sea!" Grammy Val's voice boomed in the cramped mobile home. The crowd's cheers intensified. "This is better than some fake mechanical robot animal show." Grammy Val laughed long and hard at that, and then said loudly: "This is the real deal!"

More cheers.

Though both Mica and Erin where terrified at what was happening, they held their emotions in check. The hours in captivation had allowed them to cry their eyes out, leaving them strong and somewhat prepared to make a move, but what they weren't expecting was a room full of eager onlookers to whatever depravity Grammy Val had in mind for them. Chances of escape were beginning to seem futile.

"For this evening's show, I have two specimens from the jungles of Africa. Behold, the Bengal tiger!"

Mica looked at the fabric covering his arms as if affirming that he was indeed the one in the tiger costume. What was he supposed to do? Just what did this crazy woman want of him?

Val's voice dropped as she spoke through her teeth the way someone does while in a fit of seething angry. "Roar for the crowd, tiger."

Mica looked the crazy woman in the eyes. He knew what she was capable of, but would she really harm him and his wife in front of an audience? The idea of pretending to be a tiger was such a hit to his pride. He wasn't here for anyone's entertainment. But that whip...oh, that whip could do some serious damage.

The crowd went silent as if they could taste what was about to happen, as if they knew what the consequence of not roaring nor performing would have. Grammy Val gritted her teeth, eyes deepening into a grim expression. Rage seemed to seep out of her pores.

Erin trembled harder. She licked her dry lips and swallowed hard. She said, under her breath, voice shaking, "Just roar, Mica. Just do it. Remember Danni."

That last comment hit Mica's pride. In his humiliation, he had forgotten the focal point. Do whatever had to be done to get the hell out of there, even if that meant acting like a damn animal.

"ROAR, GOD DAMN IT!" Grammy Val cracked the whip with expert precision, barely avoiding an accidental lashing of one of her patrons. "The next one rips open your flesh. Now roar, tiger. ROAR!"

Mica, fueled by the need to find his daughter and also by anger directed toward this insane woman, sucked in a deep breath and let it out in the form of something between a roar and a scream. His voice came through loud and angry and exasperated, directed at Grammy Val as if he could somehow harm her by yelling at her. It was pathetic and sad.

The crowd went nuts. Demons hid in the corners of Val's sardonic grin.

Tears welled in Erin's eyes. She blinked them away before they would cascade down her face and further give away how truly frightened she was. It was hard to be strong for Danni. Watching her husband turned into a pile of jelly made her weak in the knees. The delicate last vestiges of hope cracked like cooked filo dough.

Averting her attention for a moment, just a few seconds to not have to see Mica cowering, crying, scared to death, Erin looked out a window. She could see the glow from the hotel, the lights around the Big Top Show. They were so close, and yet so far away. So desperate. And then she saw something impossible. Her eyes opened wider, as if trying to hone her focus. Passing by the open window was a spectacular array of wild animals. The type typically seen in a zoo. The type that was once synonymous with a traveling circus. They weren't as far off as the Big Top Show, but not exactly right outside the window either. They just sort of drifted by as if being pulled by a desert wind. She recognized a tiger, a pair of elephants, a giraffe, and a lion.

"What are you looking at?" Val said.

Erin's mouth dropped. How could she be seeing this? Where were they coming from?

Grammy Val's voice remained flat and agitated as she held

back the anger that hid just beyond the surface. "I said, what are you looking at?"

Realizing that these statements were directed at her, Erin snapped her head away from the bizarre view outside the window and faced the woman of her nightmares. Grammy Val had a look on her face that was caught somewhere between anger, pity, and disgust.

"Don't look out there for help. Half of Bombay Beach is in here enjoying the show. The other half know better." Grammy Val looked out the window. "The hotel is too far away. They can't hear your screams, my little cheetah." She punctuated that statement with a crack of the whip, laying the end of it into Erin's hip.

Erin screeched at the bite of the whip and reared back defensively. Out of pure instinct, Mica made an aggressive move toward Grammy Val. Eve stepped in with a baton held high. She brought it down on his shoulder. "Back it up, tiger! BACK!"

Mica halted his approach and cowered in fear, his hands held up pleadingly, which brought a twisted grin to Eve's face.

Now, with both Mica and Erin crouched together on the floor, the crowd cheering and swilling beer, Grammy Val said, "Eve, my young apprentice, would you kindly gather up the taser. I think it's time we do something to keep these misbehaving animals in line, don't you?"

Eve nodded. "I think the taser is a great idea."

Chapter Twenty-Nine

Freedom didn't feel as sweet as Danni would have thought. Being outside didn't exactly remove the fear that the man in the hallway wasn't right behind her, or that she wouldn't see the woman with the colorful hair. She wouldn't truly feel free until she was reunited with her parents.

It was good to be outside though. Having so many other people around was comforting. These people were happy. Not a care in the world as they mingled and waited for the Big Top Show to begin. If only they knew. Danni thought about asking someone for help, but who could she trust? Surely not anyone working here. They were probably in on the whole thing. They probably knew that she was being locked in the room.

With all these people around, Danni began to feel like the world was closing in on her. Strange that even though she was just locked in a hotel room and now, out in the open, she felt even more claustrophobic. She so desperately wanted to say something, to ask someone for help, alert them of what happened to her, but she was afraid. What if she asked the wrong person? What if they took her back into the hotel? She didn't want to go back in. Even if she found her parents, she didn't want to go back in.

A commotion at the entrance to the big top tent drew Danni's attention away from searching the crowd for her parents, not that she really expected to see them there. Why would they be outside while she was locked in their hotel room?

A woman was arguing with someone at the entrance to the tent. It was clear that she didn't belong there. Her threadbare clothes were dirty and dotted with holes. Her skin was so deeply tanned she looked like she had spent time in a giant deep fryer. Streaks of gray ran through her frizzled black hair. Her face was severely wrinkled, lips dry and chapped, cracked and lined with black blood where the delicate flesh had split. Clutched in her hands was a wooden box.

There was something unsettling about standing at the rear of the crowd, as if Danni was placing herself in a position to be seen. Perhaps she would draw too much attention by not enjoying herself so animatedly like everyone else. The man lying on the floor outside her hotel room would have no trouble spotting her.

Danni continued to scan faces in search of her parents as she slowly drifted into the crowd, but she couldn't bring herself to laugh and play it off like she was having a ball. That would have looked more natural, but there was no way to deny the fear, the terror. It was amazing that she could hold it together enough not to break down and cry.

Lion strong.

"Can't you see them?" a voice said, rising above the din. The voice didn't belong, the tone very different from everyone else. "Don't you see the animals?"

That statement caught Danni's attention. She stopped and spun around, looking for the source of the voice. Who else saw animals? Or was it just some crazy person who hadn't taken their medication?

"Don't you see them? The animals? Can't you SEE?"

"Get outta here before we call the police!"

Just as Danni turned toward the commotion, a woman ran into her, nearly knocking the girl onto the ground. They locked eyes, Danni's wary and frightened, the woman's desperate and pleading. Something passed between them, like some ethereal message that none of the cheery onlookers (who were beginning to gawk at the scuffle) could understand.

The woman drew in a deep breath, a gasp of realization. "You can see."

Danni nodded.

The woman reached out, intricate box clutched in dirty hands. "Take this." She shook the box, indicating for Danni to grab it. "Free them."

In that moment the laughing and voices and cigarette girls and peanut sellers seemed to dissipate. The fear of being discovered by one of Danni's captors was forgotten. The connection was electric. No one else saw what Danni saw. No one else was lion strong.

Danni reached out her delicate hands, and the woman placed the little box in them. It was lighter than Danni had expected. She rubbed her thumbs along the sides, feeling the ridges of detailed design that had been carved there many years ago.

The sunburned woman didn't say another word. She didn't tell Danni what to do with the box, no direction, not so much as a suggestion, and yet Danni knew instinctively what she had to do. Perhaps it was something to take her mind off of her missing parents, something to get her mind off of the fear, the abandonment.

It wasn't so much that the box had some kind of electricity to it, some kind of magnetism that would lead her in the right direction. It was more mental, like messages, ethereal commands. Danni couldn't explain it, but she wasn't about to disregard the box. Somehow, she knew it was important. She could tell because she could hear the animals. Their cries swirled around her like flurries of suffering. Pained howls. Fearful screams and yells.

The woman was gone, or at least Danni hadn't seen where she'd gone off to. From the corners of her eyes Danni could see the animals. Circus animals. Desert animals. Dogs and cats. Coyotes. Birds. Their spirits rising and falling like wisps of fog. Danni saw them like a border framing her vision, but couldn't look at them directly without the images withering away. But that didn't matter. All that mattered at that moment was getting the box where it needed to be, and where it needed to be was inside the big top tent.

The box was the animals' salvation.

Danni stood in line. It hadn't occurred to her that she would need a ticket to get in. She wasn't thinking about that, wasn't thinking about what she had seen when she came out here. The woman couldn't get into the circus, so how did Danni think that she would be able to?

It didn't take all that long for the line to shorten. It wasn't until there were two people in front of Danni that she decided to pretend she was with the man in front of her. She figured she would just follow him in without looking at the person taking tickets and hope they assumed she was his daughter.

The man in front of Danni handed over one ticket to the young woman who was collecting tickets with broad smiles and good cheer at the opening to the tent. He shuffled in and Danni followed, only she was barred by the young woman's arm. "Ticket?" she said with heavy annoyance. Didn't take much to shed the fake smile.

Danni looked up, eyes wide. She opened her mouth to say something, but nothing came out.

A voice from behind said, "She's with me."

Chapter Thirty

In some ways the humiliation was worse than the physical pain, but worse than that was the realization that this could not end in anything less than murder. Though left unsaid in an experience that shunned communication between the two, Mica and Erin understood this. There were no masks concealing the identity of not only their captors, but the awful, cheering crowd. Were Mica and Erin let go, they could bring police here and have half of Bombay Beach locked up.

As the crowd of lowlifes became more drunk, their laughter became more raucous, their requests more absurd and deplorable. The sick thing was that both Grammy Val and her demented protégé Eve were more than willing to consider these requests. Some of the requests were sick, things no sane human would want to see animals participate in, much less a couple of humans, but these weren't rational people. Rational people wouldn't participate in this.

Erin, crumpled into a pile on the floor, wept. She'd just been flogged with a broom. Eve took great pleasure in this bizarre ritual. She smacked Erin in the face so hard that the bristles of the broom ripped tiny gashes that stung something terrible from intrusive sweat and dirt, although the pain wasn't quite as severe as it would have been under different circumstances, adrenalin having provided Erin with a natural anesthesia.

Whenever an act such as the broom flogging happened to Erin, Mica would become incensed, which resulted in more excitement from the crowd, and more humiliation for Mica. He knew better than to plead, but it was hard to restrain from seeking mercy. That was a natural response to being harmed. That and fighting back, and he knew what fighting back would get him.

"Our brave lion doesn't have much of a mane," Grammy Val said. Her grin was big and ridiculous, like a lopsided crescent moon. She was enjoying this too much. "He's more of a lioness, isn't he?"

The crowd cheered and whistled. Someone yelled, "Make him attack the cheetah!" Another degenerate yelled, "Pull out his teeth! Circus lions ain't got no teeth!"

Grammy Val nodded at these suggestions, but had one of her own. "What do you say, Eve, that we have a little fun with our cowardly lion?"

Eve nodded. Voice like an evil doll, she said, "What do you have in mind, Grammy Val?"

"Well, he's a coward, like I said, but he's getting a bit restless, don't you think?"

"You got that right?"

Grammy Val pursed her lips and tilted her head, examining the man standing before her in a cheap lion costume. "I can only think of one sure way to calm a lion down, one thing that will emasculate him more than he already is. Any guesses?"

The crowd spat out suggestions that ranged from the absurd to the ridiculous. Anything from braining him to sodomy to pulling his teeth (Jeremy Henderson, a toothless old buzzard himself, was adamant about that particular suggestion), but Grammy Val shook her head.

Grammy Val, the Trailer Park Ring Mistress, said one word: "Castration!"

Chapter Thirty-One

"She's with me. Here are our tickets."

Danni swiveled her head to see who had come up from behind, glad to recognize the woman she and her parents had run into a couple of times. She thought her name was Beth.

Their eyes locked and Danni knew, through some kind of instinctual sense, that she could trust this woman. Perhaps it was in the kind eyes, or maybe the concern that hid itself there in the wrinkles. In some way, Danni didn't understand, nor had the time to ponder, she knew that somehow Bette was aware of the strangeness surrounding the hotel.

The ticket taker eyed Bette suspiciously, and then ripped the ends off the tickets and let them in.

Inside the tent the fragrance of a circus was much denser. The popcorn seemed to infiltrate their nostrils with buttery love. The sweet spun cotton candy made their teeth hurt. Hotdogs and cheapo nachos had a touch of 7-11, mingling with spilled beer and strongly brewed coffee. These were people smells that often elicited gatherings and good times, but not so much at this moment for both Bette and Danni.

"Are your parents in here?" Bette asked.

Danni shook her head. Her grip on the decorative box was severe. Bette's eyes darted to the box and then back to Danni's eyes.

"What's in the box? I . . . I saw the woman. Do you know her?"

Again, Danni shook her head.

Bette's eyes slanted. "Where are your parents?"

Danni's eyes welled up, but she kept her emotions in check. She remained lion strong. "I don't know. They're missing. I was locked in our hotel room for a day. I just got out. I . . ." Danni held out the box. Her hands trembled, causing it to shiver. "I need to bring this in here. I . . ." Danni swallowed hard. Her eyes were wide, the flawless skin around them red and matted with sheen. "Touch it."

Bette was reluctant. For this moment, it was as if they were inside the circus tent alone, as if all of the people around them had faded into the background. Nothing else mattered.

Danni held the box out more fervently, but refrained from forcing it into Bette's hands. She didn't want to let go of it, couldn't, but she knew that Bette was like her. She had sensed something special about the woman from the moment she met her in the hallway.

"Have you seen the lion?" Danni asked.

At this, Bette gasped. It looked like she had learned some great and deep truth. Danni nodded and forced her lips into the slightest smile, the kind that said, *yes, it's okay, touch the box.*

An unspoken understanding spread between the two, connecting like separate beads of water on wax paper.

Bette placed one hand on the intricate wooden box and drew in a breath. As she did so, a jolt of energy shot through her arm. She trembled and drew in a jagged breath like someone in extreme cold.

Voice but a whisper in a tent full of boisterous noise, Bette said, "I feel it. And I've seen them. Not just a lion. They're everywhere."

The box insisted on pulling them as if there was some invisible line tied to it that someone across the circus tent tugged on, yet there was no slack in the pull. Danni, holding the box firmly with both of her hands, and Bette, with her hand palming the top, heeded to the pull and, by weaving through various people who didn't seem to be paying attention to anything outside of their own experience, they found themselves at the edge of the ring. The box wanted them to enter the circus ring.

"We can't do that!" Bette said. "We can't go out there."

Danni was zeroed in on the center of the ring. "I have to." With that, she continued her walk, right past the barrier that everyone else in the tent dare not pass for they knew that it was forbidden to enter the circus ring. Bette stayed behind, just watching the little girl and fearing for what was to happen next.

The ring was a large circle of dirt giving it an authentic circus feel. Intricate lighting above cast warm, unforgiving light. Voices hollered at Danni from behind, security guards and various workers who were intent on having opening night go off without a hitch, but they didn't get to Danni before she made it to the center of the ring, where the wooden box stopped its horizontal pull for a vertical pull, as if trying to draw the thing down to the ground.

Spectators in the bleachers hollered and laughed, some of them angry and yelling for the little girl to get out of the ring. Security asked for the parents, who are the parents! One of them accosted Bette, who claimed she was only an acquaintance. She told them that the poor girl's parents were missing, to which they gave a look like she was trying to explain string theory.

Danni knelt. She placed the box on the naked floor of the circus ring, a floor of dirt that must have been brought in to cover the desert sand beneath. The box seemed to lock onto the ground as if bonded by a strong cement, and suddenly the euphoric feeling of holding the box fled, replaced with an equally repellant sensation that caused Danni to see, for a split second, a crowd of skeletons surrounding her. She jumped back and lost her footing, tumbling to the ground onto her backside, which caused an eruption of laughter from the skeletons. Danni took in the macabre audience with a feeling like she had stumbled into a horror movie, and then their human forms returned as the last dregs of the box's pull evaporated.

The box trembled, and then the dirt at all sides shifted and sputtered as the box began to descend. At this, the crowd quieted as if someone had silenced them with a gunshot, as if the show they sat there waiting for had finally begun.

Chapter Thirty-Two

The waters of the Salton Sea began to ebb and flow as if some secret tide had been put in play or some giant underwater turbine had been turned on for the sole purpose of creating waves.

Water lapping at the shores increased with each pulse of the newfound tide until small waves crashed, breaking with green foam and drawing forth long-buried bones. The small waves turned into moderate waves, and the bones of countless fish and various birds washed ashore, turning the sand into an upturned graveyard, which was prevalent only a few years ago.

A low rumble emanated from somewhere in the area, perhaps the desert, perhaps the middle of the Salton Sea itself. The moderate waves increased to serious breakers, and more bones crashed upon the shore in bubbly foam and thick, brackish sediment. With the larger waves that created an entirely new shorescape came larger bones from animals that were not native to the area.

Desert sands swirled into ghostly funnels distributing sheets of sand over the road through Slab City. Dunes rumbled as earth cracked, revealing fissures from which gasses spewed forth, spraying desert sand upward in a cascading spray of granules. From the fissures, visible in the mist of desert sand were vengeful horses and coyotes, dogs and buzzards, apparitions that shifted from a natural state to a skeletal state depending on the density of the dust cloud from which they emerged.

The thick crust of paint covering the dunes of Damnation Mountain cracked and spilled sand with the occasional bones that would shoot out like projectiles. The bones ranged in size, and the various skulls that jettisoned from the damned hills were that of animals: bobcats, tigers, coyotes, cats, and more.

Asphalt cracked. The earth rumbled. A stampede of the dead gathered.

The apex rumble came from the final box, dead center in the circus tent. Yells of "earthquake! earthquake!" were shouted. People began to panic, and it was infectious. The box was gone, somewhere deep within the desert floor, its power locked with that of the other boxes creating a magical trinity, something even Katherine wasn't completely aware of when she began planting them, boxes with power the train-hopping hobo who gave her the boxes didn't inform her about. Perhaps destiny. Perhaps revenge.

At the first vibes that pulsated through the ground, Danni was on her feet and scrambling backwards toward Bette, who waited for her at the edge of the circus ring. The little girl ran into Bette's arms much to the security guards' chagrin, however, they were too absorbed in the oncoming earthquake to bother with the little girl and her magical wooden box.

"I think we should get out of here," Bette said.

Danni nodded. She looked as if the box had taken it out of her. Like the pulsating power had been feeding off of her somehow, draining some of her spirit to complete the trinity, forming ethereal fibers that connected the boxes, sand, and sea in tragedy.

Hand in hand, Bette and Danni rushed out of the circus tent, people following in their wake, rushing out for fear than something would crash down upon them, all assuming the rumble was that of a massive earthquake.

Just as they exited the circus, Danni risked a look back, concerned with what had happened, what she had done by placing the box in the center of the ring. A massive crack had split the ground, as if attempting to half the circus tent, from which circus animals emerged, led by the lion.

Danni's lion.

Chapter Thirty-Three

From the roiling waters of the Salton Sea a shape emerged through fans of water like a primordial beast. It let out a war cry and whipped its trunk around. Tigers, horses, dogs, and even snakes were flanking the ghostly elephant, slithering between hooves like quick moving wrinkles over bones and sand. Though the animals would never walk together under normal circumstances, they certainly did so in their ethereal state, as if all centered on the same task, spiritual equals.

The herd headed for the big top.

Bette and Danni couldn't believe their eyes. Of all the bizarre things that had happened to the two of them since coming to the Salton Sea, all of the strange animal sightings and hallucinations, this was beyond belief, and yet the animals roamed, stomping the ground, growling and furious.

Bette said, "Come on." She and Danni ran for a safe place away from the hotel, both shocked and unable to articulate their fear and awe. They could only watch and wonder if this was some kind of dream they would wake from. It had to be, right? Some bizarre shared nightmare.

The herd rumbled through the parking lot, crushing cars and

trucks with ease, no recoiling from pain, no concern over bodily damage. They were aglow in a gray, ethereal aura, bones showing through torn flesh, wounds of their previous life sealed over in ethereal scabs. Their eyes glowed afire.

People rushed out of the circus tent screaming, only to find themselves faced with a new, impossible horror. The herd of animals grew, coming in from all around and converging on the circus tent. There was no mercy. Elephants trampled women, men, and children alike as the herd of animals crashed into the circus, taking the massive permanent tent down like an iceberg took down the Titanic. Sparks flew from mechanical animals as they were crushed into twisted metal and flying bolts. Great wooden beams cracked and splintered. Canvas ripped. Teeth gnashed; claws swiped. Innocents were slaughtered.

Bette and Danni clutched one another tight. Danni buried her face in the crook of Bette's arm, unable to witness the destruction but also unable to prevent her ears from hearing the screams of the dying, the crashing of the tent, and the whaling cries of tormented animals that carried above it all like something tortured.

Once the tent was in shambles of twisted metal, canvas, and bloodied bodies, the animals converged on the hotel as if navigated through a hivemind. Elephants used their heads like battering rams, very unlike their normal behavior. Just as odd were the giraffes galloping and slamming into the hotel, elementals of destruction.

Surprisingly enough, it didn't take a whole lot to topple the structure. The sheer force and mass of animals was something hotels weren't built to withstand. They were an army in an unprecedented war, an army that couldn't be defeated, couldn't be harmed, and they were angry.

It was more dramatic than a controlled blast taking down a Las Vegas hotel-casino. The building fell, and the crash was deafening. Danny put her hands over her ears and clenched her eyes tight. There was no distinguishing the sounds of shattering glass, ruptured drywall, or cracking framework. It all came together in a boom that felt like an earthquake and created a massive dust cloud that swept over the entire lot the hotel had been built upon.

As the dust settled, the rumbling continued. Spectral animals wandered this way and that, some of them perhaps disoriented from the massive dust cloud, others perhaps satisfied with the state of destruction. Bette and Danni retreated from the rumbling of hooves and deep thumping of elephant feet.

"Are they coming after us?" Danni asked, her voice wavering.

Bette took a moment to answer, blinking her eyes repeatedly in an attempt to see through the dust. "I don't think so."

"Where are they going?"

"Well, it looks like they're going toward Bombay beach."

Chapter Thirty-Four

While the big top tent and the Circus Oasis Hotel were being demolished, a herd of horses, donkeys, and a random variety of animals came from the desert—a place that had become a graveyard of animals going back dozens of careless, decadent years of cruelty. They galloped together with ferocious gait, trampling over Damnation Mountain. Years worth of thick, crusted pain split and crumbled into colorful dust beneath so many eager hooves. The dunes beneath collapsed, fine sand spilling through fractured art like a ruptured hourglass.

Some of the animals lost their footing and went down, vanishing in a puff of sand and ethereal matter. The others continued their rough gallop until there was nothing left but tiny piles of sand sparkling with a glitter of various colors. All it would take was one good storm, and Damnation Mountain's evidence would disappear forever.

Those who did not fall back into eternal slumber continued forward, responding to a call only those murdered and buried in the desert and the Salton Sea could hear. They moved on some kind of otherworldly instinct, something as powerful as necromancy with the strength to pull these tortured souls from their unnatural graves, from their unnatural deaths.

As they followed the sand-strewn road, homed in on Bombay Beach, they passed a woman who sat slumped against a small dune, close enough to be harmed by the stampede, but completely ignored by the determined animal spirits. She laughed as they passed by. Laughed like she had lost her mind somewhere. Maybe tonight while delivering the final box. Maybe somewhere over the past week delivering the previous two.

Katherine Lazar's insane laughter dried up. Her eyes went wide as she stared at the passing herd. The sound of so many hooves over that deeper desert floor that was as solid as rock was like an avalanche. Their whooping cries and rumbling exhalations were a battle cry. Katherine understood this. She knew them. She remembered all that she wished she could forget. The reasons she left the family. The reasons she rode the rails and lived in so many places across the United States, always to come back here, and always to regret that decision.

After the herd passed, Katherine was left in a cloud of dissipating dust that whipped with rogue winds. It had been done. Katherine didn't know what to expect. She had no idea what she had been given the boxes of tramp art for, and she could never have dreamed up something like this.

The sound of pattering in the sand distracted Katherine from her glassy stare out over the sand where the animals had stampeded off. She shifted her head lazily. Katherine was weak. She could feel something within, something like a sickness that caused her head to burn with fever. It happened about a half an hour after she handed over the third box to that little girl. It was as if she had suddenly been ravaged by a flu that was already at its terrible peak, and she had no medicine to help. Only the ghostly stampede had taken her mind off of the throbbing therein.

A dog padded up to her through the sand. It was muted in

color, the fur matted with several columns of spinal cord visible through a tear in its neck, but Katherine recognized him immediately. It was Rascal. Even in his state, even with the blood-matted fur, he had that massive grin Katherine knew so well, that panting grin a black lab exhibits, wagging his tail excitedly. Just like old times.

Like before, Valerie Lazar tortured him in a fit of anger when Katherine spoke up against her mother. It was supposed to be an act of dominance toward Katherine, but Val enjoyed the power. She enjoyed the torture, the taking of innocent, helpless life. After Rascal was killed, Katherine left, aimless, homeless, and on the streets, or rather on the rails. She would never have thought that her mother could have gotten as bad as she did, never tortured and murdered so many animals.

Rascal leapt onto Katherine playfully and lapped at her face. This time she could feel his tongue, could smell his dog breath (something that always seemed garbage-awful in the past, but was nothing less than a miracle at the moment). Katherine stroked the matted fur and scratched him in the places that always caused his back legs to kick. Her fever was forgotten.

Laying back into the small tuft of sand, Katherine petted her dog as he lapped at her face and nuzzled her with his muzzle. She closed her eyes. A tear traveled down her face creating a wet trail across her dusty cheek. A weight was lifted, and then Katherine stood and walked with Rascal to gently fade into a swirl of desert sand.

Chapter Thirty-Five

Mobile homes tended to have two doors, one that was considered the front door that led into the living room and another in the kitchen that typically led to a covered parking area that most people used as their front door. The entire time Mica and Erin had been humiliated inside the Lazar family mobile home they had an eye on the kitchen door. Just given a half a moment to run, they would have taken it, but with so many patrons sitting there watching gleefully as they were forced to do ridiculous things, there was no opportunity for escape.

Until the rumbling that had been heard off in the distance intensified.

The flimsy walls shook something violent. Those in attendance dropped their popcorn sacks and beers and scrambled, fearing an earthquake. They headed for the door in the living room, the closest one they had access to, getting caught in the doorframe like a bunch of teenagers fleeing a kegger after talk of police. Then the walls split. Rather than creating an easier getaway, the people of Bombay Beach were torn apart by any number of animals. Screams erupted. The lucky ones made it out, but there was no telling what awaited them outside.

At this, Mica tapped Erin on the shoulder and motioned toward the door in the kitchen. The animal attack had come from the other end of the mobile home. The opportunity they had been looking for presented itself, but they had to be quick.

Without thinking, they ran for that door. Mica fumbled with the fake paw gloves that were affixed to his arms, but managed to open the door. Had it been locked, there was no way he would have been able to open it. Risking a look back, Erin saw that Grammy Val was after them. She screamed something, but her voice was rivaled by the mayhem of the rampaging animals and the screams of Bombay Beach.

Erin yelled, "RUN!"

Mica paused for a second, processing the one-word command that barely entered his eardrum through the destruction of the mobile home that resembled a microcosmic war scene. Erin took her own advice and booked it, passing her husband. She looked back as she ran to make sure that he was with her, and then slowed her run when she saw Grammy Val standing at the doorway. The woman cracked her whip, and it lashed Mica across his face and chest. He recoiled and let out an agonized scream. Grammy Val laughed, though it couldn't be heard. She looked mad with the dust of destruction billowing around her.

The mobile home was hit with more violent shakes. Grammy Val turned at the sound of her granddaughter's scream. A lion pounced on the girl, smacking her around with its massive paws like she was a dummy. The lion looked at Val and snarled, then lunged at Eve, ripping its teeth into her throat. Shaking its head vigorously, it ripped out her larynx, and then went in for more, this time severing her spine. Holding her head by a nub of vertebrae, it swung the head back and forth until it became freed and launched a colorful ball of dyed hair and fresh blood across the room.

Several galloping horses converged upon Elric, their hooves

dimpling his body into a bag of broken bones and pulped meat. Snakes slither by and nipped at him. Dogs paid tribute with bites of their own and even a lifted leg here and there.

Other bodies were strewn about, torn and punctured, bloody and lifeless from no discernible cause of death. This was a crime scene no forensics analyst or CSI people would be able to piece together.

While Grammy Val's attention was distracted, Mica and Erin ran. By the time the woman turned around and let out another crack of her whip, they were too far away for her to reach.

That's when the rumbling intensified. The mobile home completely collapsed as the elephants came through. Grammy Val remembered them vividly. They had been her great triumph after the original hotel was closed down. She had garnered so much power in taking them down, more so than the lions. Just the sheer size of the elephants made their torture and murder a powerful thing.

But now the tables were turned. The elephants, two of them, were furious and they had one sight in their previously gentle, now burning eyes. In a tactical move, both elephants attacked, lowering their massive heads and lifting up, impaling Val with their tusks. They stood on opposite sides, one tusk piercing her upper torso, near her right shoulder, the other piercing her pelvis. The elephants pulled in opposite direction and eviscerated the sick old woman. Her agonized screams were cut off, and her body strewn on the ground to be nibbled and pecked and paid homage to by all of her past ghosts.

Chapter Thirty-Six

They were disoriented, but running toward the glow off in the distance. It had to be the hotel. There was nothing else out there in the desert that could justify such a massive light source. In their haste to get away, Mica tripped and fell hard to the ground. Erin heard him stumble and turned to see her husband struggling with the ridiculous animal outfit he had on, sweaty and contorted around his body like a bizarre straitjacket. She crouched beside him. They looked back again but only saw the destruction of so many mobile homes. The one where they had been held was nothing but a pile of rubble. Various animals wandered about. The rage they seemed to possess only moments ago had appeared to flee. In a strange twist of reality, some of them looked like mirages, figments of imagination that faded into nothing, drifting away with clouds of dusts that lifted from the ruins like heat waves on scorching asphalt.

"We've got to get to Danni," Erin said. "She must be terrified."

Mica just nodded, licking his lips and staring off toward Bombay Beach.

They both turned, Erin ready to help Mica up, when they were confronted by a tiger. The couple froze. Erin remembered something about standing perfectly still when in the presence of a bear and wondered if the same went for predatory felines. Probably not. She had also heard that mountain lions were stalkers, smarter than your average bear. A tiger was more likely to fall into that category.

The tiger breathed heavily, sounding like a purr mixed with a low growl. Something terrifying. It approached. Mica and Erin held one another tight, prepared for the worst. The tiger got closer, sniffed them, and then lapped their faces with its sandpaper tongue. Then the tiger dissipated, its ethereal fibers releasing into the atmosphere.

Erin looked into Mica's eyes. They were both trembling, their faces smeared with dirt and tears. What could possibly come next?

"The hotel," Mica said, and Erin nodded in agreement.

They stood up and headed toward the flickering light. Deep down, they knew it wasn't right, but it wasn't until they ascended the massive dune that separated Bombay beach from the property the Circus Oasis was built upon that they realized why the light was inconsistent and flickering. The hotel was no longer standing. Now it was a flaming pile of debris.

Erin's mouth went into an O, words unable to be projected. Glistening eyes reflected the bright orange tide of flames.

Mica said, "She's . . . is she in there?"

Erin just shook her head in disbelief.

Mica's eyes welled. "Our baby girl . . ."

"Maybe . . ." Head swiveling. "No, she can't be."

Mica couldn't deny the tears that came forth. They had been there for a long time. He had to be strong inside Grammy Val's house, and now he could let them go. He collapsed to his knees and sobbed.

Erin said, "Shhh, wait."

Mica looked up through teary eyes seeing the world through rainy windshields.

"I hear something," she said. "People."

There were faint screams and hollering voices.

Mica stood up, wiped his eyes so he could see. "There's people down there. Maybe Danni got out!"

They descended the Circus Oasis side of the dune that had been put there to block out the bad view of Bombay Beach. As they walked through the backside of the massive lot, people passed by, some covered in blood, limping, pressing hands to deep wounds that needed medical attention. Others hollered for loved ones. Some were burned. Most were crying or had faces slathered in tears and soot and sand. This was the aftermath of a disaster.

Mica and Erin looked at every child they saw, hoping one of them would be Danni. The fear of some violent circus animal was gone. All that mattered was Danni, and she didn't seem to be in this sparse crowd of wanderers.

"Danni!" Mica hollered. Erin did the same.

They called for their little girl until their voices were raw. Others called out for loved ones without answer. Desperation could be heard in those voices. Finally, sirens whaled off in the distance.

People regarded Mica and Erin with wide, horrified eyes. Looks of disgust and awe and confusion. The warmth within the animal suits was enough for them to want to shed them, but they couldn't do that. Standing in their underwear would earn them just as many strange stares.

"Mommy!"

Erin whipped around at a little girl's voice. She saw a weeping mother embrace her daughter. Erin just shook her head. She too wept and Mica held her close, stroking her frazzled hair, his hand now freed of the paw glove that he'd been forced to wear.

"We'll find her. I know we will."

Erin shook her head, rubbing her forehead over the fur and zipper over Mica's chest. "No," she wept. "No, we won't. She was in the hotel. I know it. She was in there. Waiting for us to come back."

Mica whispered, "You don't know that."

Erin pulled away from Mica. Her eyes were on fire, raging in a moment of fear and hurt. "Well, she isn't out here," she snapped.

Mica nodded. "We don't know that. There's still a chance. Believe me."

"Believe you? You who lied to me for so long about, about working when you weren't even looking for a job. We should have never come out here. We should have stayed home. We—"

"Mommy!"

Erin stopped mid-sentence. This time she didn't swivel toward the voice for fear of seeing another lucky parent reunited with their child. She couldn't bare to see that again. She couldn't lose hope again. But then she saw Mica's eyes. He was looking over her shoulder. His eyes lit up. His jaw dropped, and she knew.

"Danni?" Erin whispered, looking into her husband's eyes as if she could see her little girl through the reflections off his retinas. He just nodded.

"Mommy, daddy!"

Erin turned, a breath caught in her throat, tears afresh spilled down her cheeks, battling for purchase through grime and sand. Through obscured vision, she could see a little girl, and for a split second she thought the woman next to her must have been another mother, that this was another lost hope. She wiped her eyes and saw clearly that it was Danni running toward her. She recognized the woman as Bette from the hotel, standing there like a guardian angel.

Erin and Mica, clothed like a sad cheetah and lion, embraced their daughter.

"Oh my god," Erin said. "I can't believe it."

"It's so good to see you," Mica said. "We thought we'd lost you."

After many tears shed and an exchange of pleasantries followed by Danni's brief, yet thorough explanation of what had happened to her, Mica asked, "How did you recognize us?"

Danni's face dropped. Her chin trembled. "I thought I wasn't ever going to see you again. I thought . . . When I woke up alone in the room . . ." She opened her mouth and words would not come forth. Tears did, and they embraced again. Danni whispered in her father's ear, "I saw the lion costume, and I knew. I just knew it had to be you." Mica's grip tightened around his daughter, and then she added: "Lion strong."

Epilogue

After a late night of police reports and sharing survival stories that seemed to get more daring with each telling, Bette decided she would drive home rather than find a motel to hole up in for the night. After what she had been through, she was wired and wouldn't be able to sleep anyhow.

She exchanged phone numbers with Mica and Erin, but knew that it would be unlikely anything came of it. They were overly thankful that she had been watching out for Danni, but she was quick to tell them that Danni was a special little girl and mostly watched out for herself.

News crews showed up, probably tipped off by someone for a few greenbacks. Bette was interviewed on camera, but had no idea and no real interest to find out if any of the footage was used on the news (although she would see herself on CBS, FOX, and NBC the following day when the story broke nationally).

Bette would get home just as Dennis was getting up. He would be shocked to hear her story. She wouldn't exaggerate her heroism as some people had been doing. She would just tell him what happened. Maybe leave out the ghostly animals that she couldn't get out of her head, because those kind of details would cause Dennis to think she was out of her mind.

But she'd seen the elephants. Tigers. Giraffes.

She didn't tell the news outlets about that. Didn't write anything about that in the statement she made for the police. It was too crazy. Too unbelievable. She didn't want anyone thinking she was some loony old woman. Everyone had seen it, but how could that be? Some kind of mass hypnosis? Something in the water? That sometimes truth was, in fact, stranger than fiction?

She wanted to tell Dennis, but how could she? Any way she thought of the conversation in her mind, she sounded crazy. People looked at you funny if you claimed to see a human ghost, much less a hoard of animal spirits destroy an entire hotel.

It would be easier to tell him about the cancer. That was what really mattered anyway. The incidents at the Salton Sea would soon fade from the headlines as other catastrophes took their place.

The cancer was real.

As Bette sat in her car in front of her house, waiting for a light to come on indicating that Dennis was awake, she looked at the little slip of paper with both Mica and Erin's cell phone numbers. That Danni was a special little girl.

Nothing would probably come of it, but Bette would make that call. See how they were all doing.

Talk to Danni and see how her lion was doing.

The End

9 781959 205173